BEARCANO

BEARCANO

LINDSAY MERCOVICH

MERCO
MULTIMEDIA

Lindsay Mercovich

Thank you to all those who support my ideas, no matter how weird or fanciful they get.

For Gordon

CHAPTER 1

Jun Wei stared out the window of the helicopter as it flew across the forest, admiring the golden glow slipping over the mountains as the last moments of sunset faded.

It had been some time since he had last been in America, having previously lived and studied here at the insistence of his father. He had been instructed to gain a strong knowledge of western business practices if he was to ever be included in the family business and eventually take over his fathers' position at the head of the corporation.

Those formative years seemed like a different lifetime, as he had returned to Beijing several years ago to claim his place within the company. The Lingzhi Corporation was a multinational biotech company which had grown from humble beginnings in cosmetics and consumer goods.

Over the years, thanks to his father's shrewd business dealings, the company had expanded to bio-medical, pharmaceutical, industrial and military technology.

They had offices in multiple countries around the world, growing their network of associates and clients with every business deal and each new product on the market.

A finger in every pie, Jun Wei thought to himself as he mused about his current position and latest assignment.

As he had progressed up the corporate ladder and into his father's good graces, only then did he start to learn more about the corporations more *below board* operations.

Military-grade weapons development, bioengineering with no ethical oversight, and trade within the black market. All were highly lucrative, providing interesting business opportunities all over the world and new markets to exploit.

The Corporation had a long and storied relationship with the rich and affluent back in China.

There has always been a large demand for the more exotic types of medicine and the governing elite and crime bosses were willing to pay top dollar for anything that will allow them to maintain their power and extend their lives, in a desperate bid to build their dynasties before their influence waned with age.

Old men and their magic potions, he thought to himself, *more status symbols than anything else, but if they wanted to pay through the nose, that's their business.* All Jun Wei cared about was the money they paid and his father's approval.

That is why he had jumped at the chance to embark on this journey, to tour one of the corporations secret black site laboratories and report back on their progress.

It seemed like an easy assignment to him, and it was somewhat nice to be back in the States after such a long absence.

Jun Wei looked around the spacious interior of the aircraft, a customised version of the Changhe Z-18 that the Chinese military used.

This one had been modified for corporate use, which include a plush interior and even a bar.

The Helicopter could comfortably fit the entire corporation's board of directors inside yet was empty apart from Jun Wei and the pilot. Jun Wei liked this type of special treatment and took it as a good sign of his father's opinion of him.

The helicopter's engines had been customised he was told and could fly with a minimum of noise. Jun Wei had noticed the curious shape of the rotor blades as they first boarded, the dull thrum of the rotor barely audible from the inside.

Jun Wei poured himself a drink from the bar, a 1969 Glenrothes single malt scotch whisky, and took a sip.

He grabbed the bar to steady himself as the helicopter banked sharply and started to climb. They had been flying low to avoid any possible detection. The aircraft's black silhouette rendering it all but invisible against the darkening sky.

I guess the point of a secret base is that it stays a secret, Jun Wei thought as he swirled the dark liquor around his glass before taking another sip.

Looking out the window he could see a large mountain approaching, a dormant volcano he had been told, and judging by its size it was a good thing it was no longer active.

Mount Arktos as it was known, dominated the landscape and dwarfed the town that lay at the base of the mountain. From his position, he could see the whole town, the lights from buildings standing out like a beacon as the last hints of sunlight sunk below the horizon.

There was just enough light left that he could make out the large lake near the centre of the town, Lake Ursa, the namesake of the town that had sprung up around it.

The town seemed like any of the other mid-western towns he had heard about in his youth.

Growing up privileged in Beijing, his father had decided that Jun Wei was to be educated in the West, to not only prepare him for the cutthroat world of business, but to start learning from a young age as much about how their corporate rivals in America operated.

Jun Wei had attended Harvard University, a position that was not earned through any academic prowess on his part, but solely due to his father's influence.

He spent those years living the American dream as he called it, non-stop parties, drugs, booze and women.

Those had been good times, the first real time he could explore the type of person he was, and wanted to be, without his father's stern eye looking over him.

But that all ended, news of his party boy antics finally reaching home. Some of his father's goons turned up at the university one day, packed him up and send him back to Beijing before he could even say goodbye to his friends.

He had always resented his father for that, and the shame he had felt when he saw his father's disapproving glare.

The last few years he had kept his head down, trying to prove his worth to his father once more. There were many others looking to wear the crown and they were prepared to step over him to get it.

The town was a popular tourist destination he had heard, the natural hot springs by the lake and towering forests surrounding the town made it ideal for campers and other such naturists.

The sleepy little town was probably full of friendly locals who knew each other's names, a far cry from the bustling cities he was used to back home.

Perhaps when his business here was concluded he could investigate it further.

The helicopter continued its ascent, keeping close to the side of the mountain. Jun Wei felt a surge of panic as he could no longer see very well out of the windows and into the night sky.

He knew that they were dangerously close to the side of the mountain, a manoeuvre designed to further mask their radar signature from anyone who might be watching.

He breathed deeply and continuously assured himself that the pilot had done this many times before and knew what he was doing. As he repeated that to himself like a mantra, they reached the lip of the volcano.

Despite being described as dormant, the volcano still had quite a lot of activity going on. Heat and volcanic gases still rose from the mouth, making it a no-fly zone.

The helicopter had been designed to be perfectly airtight to allow it to pass through these toxic gases unharmed, its engines modified to allow it to remain functional.

Any other aircraft would stall and crash under circumstances like these, but the pilot flew confidently over the top and down into the crater.

As the helicopter slowly lowered, Jun Wei could see a glow coming from down below. It seemed insane to place any type of facility here, but it did help to hide their activities.

The Dragon's Lair as it has been designated was starting to live up to its name.

Midway down the chasm, Jun Wei could see the facility, seemingly hovering over the glowing bowels of the volcano. He had been briefed on its layout prior to his departure, but it was still a startling piece of engineering to behold.

The facility was a self-contained habitat, internally sealed from the harsh environment and toxic fumes it was enveloped in. It was anchored to the internal walls of the volcano by large metal cables, the main facility hung in the middle like some sort of fat spider sitting in its web.

Below the facility, long tubes descended into the lava flows beneath it. Heat exchangers that powered the entire structure on geothermal energy.

Completely off-grid and self-contained, the ambient heat helped mask any thermal signature which may be picked up by intrusive satellites.

The complex was broken up into several hubs containing laboratories and living facilities for the staff of over 100 scientists and engineers. Long twisting corridors connecting each of the hubs, stuck out from the main facility and hung over the void.

Jun Wei imagined the facility a bustling hive of his father's most dedicated workers, all scurrying around in a giant ant colony.

A sense of anxiety gnawed at his stomach, as a wave of claustrophobia washed over him. He was in a flying metal box, slowly descending towards a cramped building, dangling precariously over one of the most inhospitable environments imaginable. *What could go wrong?*

The helicopter continued its descent, the landing lights of a helipad on the roof of the complex became visible.

"Touchdown in 20 seconds", said the pilot over the intercom.

Jun Wei nodded to himself and walked toward the back of the helicopter. There was a large storage locker containing several protective suits.

As part of his briefing, he had been advised of the need for protective gear when entering and leaving the facility. Breathing apparatus and a protective suit were required to survive the 100-metre walk from the landing pad to the main doors.

When he had inquired why such measures were required and why they hadn't just built some sort of contained airlock, he had been advised it was an extra layer of security needed to not only stop people getting in, but to potentially stop people getting out.

Jun Wei had heard about whistle-blowers working in these black sites before, but this seemed extreme even to him.

What exactly was going on in there he wondered? He guessed he would find out soon enough as he affixed the final parts of his protective suit.

The quiet thrum of the helicopter's rotors died down and the helicopter became completely silent. All Jun Wei could hear was his own breathing inside his helmet, and the buzz of small electric fans circulating cool air around his suit.

After checking everything on the suit was correct as he had been briefed to do so, he opened a sealed door towards the back of the aircraft and stepped into a confined airlock.

Signalling to the pilot via intercom he was ready, a brief warning alarm sounded, and the side door of the helicopter depressurised and opened.

Stepping out of the door, Jun Wei could feel the heat even through the protective suit.

The inside of the volcano looked like nothing he could have ever imagined. The glow from the lava flows below illuminating the hazy fog of the toxic air. He could now see that The Dragon's Lair was an extremely fitting name.

The ground in front of him lit up with tiny markers directing him toward an open airlock across from the landing pad.

His pilot soon joined him by his side, clad in his own protective suit, as the door to the helicopter hissed close.

He had been advised earlier that it was uncommon for helicopters to remain on-site, their arrival only for the delivery of personnel and supplies.

I guess it helps dissuade anyone who may have ideas about leaving, he thought to himself, silently thankful that they had made this one small concession for his benefit. He felt it would not take long for him to go stir crazy in a place like this if he didn't think he could ever leave when he wanted to.

The airlock door slid closed behind them, and the room filled with a whooshing sound of industrial fans as they vented the toxic air and replaced it with something more breathable.

Jun Wei could feel his suit cooling down as sweat dripped down his neck. A green light and a gentle beep signalled that it was now safe to remove their protective gear.

As Jun Wei and his pilot placed their protective gear on storage racks, the interior airlock door slid open.

A lean man, who looked to be in his sixties, with thinning grey hair and thick-rimmed glasses stood on the other side. He was clad in a long white lab coat over the top of a 3-piece suit, Italian leather shoes polished to a mirror finish.

"Greetings, I am Professor Yong Zhi, the head researcher and facility overseer," said the man as he extended his hand.

"We are most honoured to receive you, and to show you the great strides we have been making here," he said with a smile.

Jun Wei shook the man's hand, which was surprisingly firm for a man of his age. The Professor was smiling but there was a subtle look of contempt in his eyes.

Obviously, Jun Wei's position in the company did not impress him very much.

"You must be in need of freshening up after your long trip," he said, "and I would be most happy to give you a full tour of the facility…"

"Actually…" interjected Jun Wei, asserting his own power over the older man.

"I'd prefer if we could just get down to business".

He had been here less than 5 minutes and he was already starting to feel claustrophobic in the brightly lit, stark white narrow corridors of the facility. Despite the location of the facility, it felt cold and sterile, like a hospital.

They walked down the main corridor and Jun Wei noticed dozens of labs next to one another, the researchers all engrossed in their work. Not a single one stopped to look at them as they passed by.

It was an impressive, well-run facility by the looks of things, he was sure his father would be happy to hear, but the details of what he was actually there to check on still alluded him.

The Professor must have sensed this as he turned to Jun Wei as they headed down a corridor towards a large lab.

"You must be wondering what goes on here?" he said, "I'm sure a lot of the details were not shared, as it is a matter of security that we keep our research here private".

They walked into a large lab, many researchers busied themselves with their work, monitoring various computer displays and taking notes. This appeared to be a central hub of activity for them.

Jun Wei looked at the monitors as he passed by, 3D models of DNA strands and complex mathematics covered them, nothing that made a single bit of sense to him.

The Professor walked over to a large centrifuge and removed one of the vials. The long vial contained a silvery-white solution inside, the light glinted off it as the solution seemed to shift within the vial of its own accord.

"This is BC-2044", said the Professor with pride in his voice, "the latest in a long series of trials we have been conducting here".

"This will be one of our first major tests, which is what you are here to witness and report on", he said as he handed the vial to Jun Wei, the vial warm to the touch.

"Ok, but what does it do?" said Jun Wei as he inspected the vial, small silvery flecks in the solution seemingly reacting to his touch.

"Restores life" responded the Professor with a smile.

"What you have in your hands is the pinnacle of decades of research in genetic engineering, molecular biology and nanotechnology." He continued.

"Billions of dollars of investments and my life's work."

The Professor gently took the vial from Jun Wei and marvelled at it.

"We have constructed microscopic entities, that are a perfect fusion of biology and technology, a techno-organic nanomachine based on the tardigrade."

He looked at the confused expression on Jun Wei's face and directed his attention to a nearby monitor.

The monitor displayed a 3D model of a nanomachine, that looked like a small six-legged bug. The display showed the nanomachine next to a cell which was twice its size.

The 3D animation showed the tiny robot deploying a variety of tools, as it set about modifying the cell. What it was actually doing to it, Jun Wei could not tell.

"The tardigrade, known colloquially as the *water bear* is a microscopic animal with incredible resistance to the most extreme environments," said the Professor.

"They can survive in sub-zero temperatures, the vacuum of space, and being blasted with radiation. They could even survive in the scorching depths of this very volcano."

"At the heart of those tiny creatures is a will to survive, a will to adapt and overcome. It is this trait we wish to master."

"Our nanomachines can be infused into another organism, with the goal to imbue them with similar protective traits as well as extreme regenerative capabilities".

"Cells are vulnerable to damage from infections, pollutants, environmental stress, and aging," said the Professor.

"Imagine something that could not only rebuild damaged cells almost as fast as they are damaged, but could alter the cells to protect them from further damage, a *'what doesn't kill you, makes you stronger'* type situation if you will."

Placing the gleaming vial back in the centrifuge, the Professor walked across the lab to three large windows, each with large heavy-duty shutters firmly closed.

Typing a quick command into a nearby console, the shutters on all three windows opened, revealing what looked to be holding cells of some kind.

Jun Wei approached one of the windows and stopped short as he saw what was within.

The first cell contained a black bear, which reared up on its hind legs in response to the opening shutter.

Even classified as a small bear, it stood nearly two metres tall. It made a soft grunt and crouched back down on all fours, unable to see the researchers through the one-way glass window.

In the next cell was the largest animal Jun Wei had ever seen this close before. A nearby monitor displayed the name *'Kodiak bear'* along with information about its vitals.

Shambling around its cramped cell, it was nearly as tall on all fours as the black bear was standing up. Jun Wei stood staring mouth agape as the beast settled back down on the floor.

The Professor, apparently pleased by the shocked look on Jun Wei's face, ushered him to the last window.

A large brown bear, not as large as the last but still terrifyingly massive stood in the cell, its status monitor identifying it as *'Ursus Arctos Horribilis'*, a Grizzly Bear.

Nose pressed up against the glass, fogging it up with each snort of its massive nostrils, it stared intently through the glass, and as Jun Wei felt, into his soul.

"Can it see us?" Jun Wei asked nervously.

"Probably not, but it most likely can smell us" replied the Professor, completely at ease.

"This particular specimen has given us quite a deal of trouble, haven't you?" said the Professor as he tapped on the glass.

The bear grunted its reply and placed a paw up on the window, the paw was larger than the Professor's head.

Jun Wei inched back from the window as he contemplated just how strong that glass really was.

"I think we have our first candidate," said the Professor.

"Prep it for surgery."

CHAPTER 2

Jun Wei could not help but stare in awe at the bulky frame of the massive grizzly splayed out on the operating table. The bear had been sedated, removed from its holding pen and wheeled on a gurney to an adjoining lab.

Watching alongside the Professor, behind the safety glass of the laboratory's observation room, he watched as the bear was winched off the gurney and placed on its back on the operating table. Its limbs tightly locked down by restraints and a mask placed over its snout, delivering a strong anaesthetic.

One of the lab technicians, decked head to toe in surgical gear, walked over to a centrifuge in the corner of the room and picked up one of the vials, its contents shimmering like the vial Jun Wei had seen previously.

The technician placed the vial into a device that looked like some sort of gun but with a large, sinister looking needle sticking out the front.

The Professor started to narrate the procedure at this point, "...as you can see, the serum is injected directly into the subject's heart and brain stem for maximum dispersal through the circulatory and nervous system."

He waved his hand towards some displays showing various biometric data as he continued, "The assimilation process takes only a matter of minutes, as the nanomachines take up residence in the subject's muscle tissue, organs and bone marrow."

Displays in the observation room showed a 3D representation of the animal's internal structure, as a small medical scanner moved meticulously over the sedated grizzly.

Digital readouts on the displays showed green lights across the board, as the assimilation process completed.

The Professor pushed an intercom button on the wall next to the viewing window.

"All signs are stable, proceed with procurement" he said with a tremble of excitement in his voice.

Jun Wei watched with morbid fascination as the surgeons cut into the bear's abdomen, slicing open from groin to sternum, and pinning back large folds of flesh with all manner of clamps.

"I'm surprised there isn't much blood" he said, eyes fixed on the open body cavity of the bear.

"The serum is already starting its work" replied the Professor. "The nanomachines have reacted to the damage by sealing the blood vessels."

"Their primary function is to ensure homeostasis, even in the most challenging of situations."

The Professor pointed to a monitor displaying the bear's vital signs. "Heartrate, blood pressure, oxygen saturation levels are all within normal ranges."

"The nanomachines are interfacing with the subject's nervous system and with each other, coming up with new solutions to maintain homeostasis and keep the host alive."

Jun Wei looked away from the monitor and back to the operation just as the surgeons removed what appeared to be the animal's liver.

Looking back at the vitals display, there was no change at all. The Professor maintained his composure as a small smile crept onto his face.

"Remove the heart" he said into the intercom.

The surgeon's picked up their scalpels and start working away. Within a few minutes one of the surgeon's lifted the large pulsating mass from the creature's chest and placed it on a nearby tray.

Everyone in the room stopped to stare as the heart continued to contract and expand in a steady rhythm.

"Fascinating" said the Professor, his eyes locked on the beating heart.

"Even removed from the body altogether, the organ is still trying to operate."

A lab technician picked up the tray and placed the slowly pulsing heart into a chilled container.

Looking at the displays, Jun Wei was astounded, the animal's vitals were still strong. Blood pressure, heart rate, oxygen saturation all still within normal limits, *but how could this be?* he wondered.

"How is it still alive with no heart?" he said.

"The nanomachines are adapting already to the removed organs by manually moving blood around the body. They are extracting oxygen directly from the air and transporting it to cells" replied the Professor.

A moment later, a large set of lungs was placed on another tray, still inflating and deflating of their own accord as they were carried off for cold storage.

The display monitors emit a beep as vital signs start to drop. The Professor stared at the screens, then clapped his hands in triumph as the numbers climbed back up to their previous levels.

Soon the surgeons had removed most of the animal's vital organs, yet it remained alive.

Jun Wei was aware of the '*procurement*' of exotic animal parts that were favoured by the elite back home, *could this be all part of some renewable source of black-market organ harvesting*?

"Now to begin phase two of the trial," said the Professor. "Start reducing the sedative and bring in the transfusion material."

Jun Wei noticed a silvery fluid starting to seep out of the animal, almost like blood but thicker, like mercury from a broken thermometer.

"The next phase is to test the regenerative capabilities of the nano-machines," said the Professor.

"The sedatives are impeding cellular repair, so we need to bring the subject back to a state of consciousness. Of course, this will be quite painful for the subject, but should be what we need to trigger the desired response" he continued.

"This part is key. We will provide a transfusion of fats and proteins to the animal. The nanomachines will use this material to build new cellular structures to repair what has been removed."

The Professor pressed up close to the window, eager to see what happened next. The nanomachines had proven successful in keeping the animal alive despite a remarkable amount of trauma to its vital organs, but could they undo the damage and restore the animal to health?

"We are on the cusp of the greatest achievement in medical science known to man" said the Professor, almost giddy.

"We will not only be able to hold back death, but to conquer it, reverse it..."

"Ah...Sir" one of the surgeons said, their voice crackling over the intercom. "The regeneration process has already begun..."

"Catabolism of existing tissue?" The Professor responded.

"Negative" responded the surgeon

"The regrowth doesn't appear to be organic; it is almost metallic in appearance."

The surgeon poked at the rapidly regenerating tissue with a scalpel, pushing hard to cut into the metallic flesh. Removing the scalpel to make a second incision, the surgeon could see the blade was missing, as if it had been dissolved.

The surgeons and medical staff shared looks of confusion with each other, as a groaning noise filled the air. Over the intercom, Jun Wei and the Professor could hear a screeching sound, like metal tearing.

A moment later, the operating table collapsed under the weight of the bear.

From where Jun Wei was standing, the metal operating table look like it had been dissolved by acid. The previously smooth surface now pocked and melted.

Everyone in the laboratory as well as those in the observation room, stood transfixed as the grizzly slowly started to rise from the remains of the table it had previously been securely restrained on.

The bear let out a low growl as it stood up on its hind legs. Towering over everything in the laboratory, the beast must have been at least two and a half metres tall.

Jun Wei felt his blood run cold as he could see directly into the still gaping chest cavity of the animal, a new metal heart beating furiously.

Nobody breathed as the bear sniffed the air and stared the medical staff and surgeons down.

Jun Wei held his breath and watched as one of the technicians inched over to a nearby table and picked up what looked to be some sort of cattle prod.

Jun Wei watched, frozen in shock as the technician crept slowly towards the bear from behind, stun prod in hand.

The bears ears twitched, and it turned towards the approaching man. The technician froze for a moment before squeezing the trigger on the prod. Electricity arced out of the tip, but the technician had barely raised it towards the bear as it lashed out.

The bear's paw connected with the man's head and shoulder, claws raking downwards. Jun Wei watched in horror as the technician's head and neck tore open in a gush of blood. His head was nearly torn completely off apart from a few tendons and scraps of flesh on one side keeping it attached, as the man's body went limp and crashed to the floor.

Panic filled the laboratory like an explosion, people scrambled out of the way as the bear turned back towards them and charged.

One young scientist could only manage a short sharp screech as the bear bit down on her head, the skull providing little resistance for its powerful jaws as it popped like an over-ripe melon.

As it rag-dolled her body to the side, the bear charged two more technicians trying to put a surgical table between themselves and the rampaging animal.

The table provided very little resistance as the bear clamped its jaws down on the arm of one man, while knocking the second man to the ground and pinning him with a massive paw.

With a flick of its head, the man in the bear's jaws went flying across the room, what was left of his arm still held firmly in its mouth.

The second man let out a blood curdling scream as the bear bit down into his stomach, loops of intestines pulling away as it lifted its head.

The remaining two surgeons used the moment of distraction to run across the room towards the laboratory doors.

The grizzly turned and gave chase, surprisingly fast for a creature of its size.

One of the scientists punched in a code on a console next to the door. The door let out a hiss as the door seal broke on the room.

From the observation room, the Professor pulled a lever on a control console on the wall. The laboratory door slid shut again, to the cries of the scientists as the bear charged towards them, mouth open.

Jun Wei felt vomit rise in the back of his throat and his legs felt weak like they wanted to collapse, as he watched the bear pull apart the two men trapped in the room.

The bear walked slowly, almost casually back to the middle of the room, to continue eating the technician it had previously disembowelled.

"You...trapped them in there" Jun Wei said quietly as he swallowed hard, fighting back the nausea.

"We had to contain the danger" responded the Professor dispassionately.

"At least it is trapped in there and we can recapture it. Had it gotten out of the lab it could have done an untold amount of damage to this entire facility."

A minute later the security response team arrived. The team stood there, shocked at the carnage in the laboratory.

The Professor hit the door override switch once more and the laboratory door slid open.

The security team filed into the room and fanned out.

The Grizzly grunted a warning at the men, as it prepared itself to attack once again.

The team leader silently waved a hand gesture at two of his men, armed with shotguns who quickly aimed and fired their weapons at the bear.

Barbed darts fired from their weapons and thudded into the bear's thick hide. A crackling sound filled the air as the taser slugs discharged into bear's body.

The Grizzly roared and staggered a few steps before being hit with another volley of taser rounds.

Another of the security team, armed with a rifle took aim and fired. A tranquiliser dart hitting the bear in the neck.

The security team cautiously backed up as the bear jerked and twitched in a vain attempt to walk, white foam dripped from its blood-stained mouth.

The security team leader, approached the bear as it slumped to the floor and drew his Desert Eagle pistol from his holster, pointing it at the animal's head.

"I want it alive Major...", the Professors voice crackled over the intercom.

Soon the incapacitated animal was firmly strapped to another gurney and ready to be moved.

That type of military precision would have been useful ten minutes ago when all those people were being slaughtered, Jun Wei thought to himself.

The grizzly was rushed quickly from the laboratory and back to the holding cells, the sedatives wearing off once more, just as it was secured.

The Grizzly paced inside the confines of its cell, stopping to inspect the wounds along its abdomen, now completely healed up as patches of gleaming metal poked through its fur.

The two other bears were soon returned to their own cells. Having already been dosed with the serum, their surgeries had been cancelled just in time, avoiding a repeat incident as word of the tragedy spread.

Back in the main laboratory, Jun Wei stood well back from the windows of the animal's cells, given what he had just witnessed. The blood and gore still thick in the Grizzly's fur, as it stared intently out the one-way glass.

The room was quiet apart from the small sobs from facility staff as they tried to come to terms with what had happened to their friends and colleagues.

As Jun Wei, the Professor and a few senior scientists moved into a nearby boardroom for a debriefing, the Professor stared intently at the results from the tests.

"This was...unexpected" he said quietly.

"Yeah, I'm pretty sure everyone being torn apart by a bear wasn't part of the experiment" said Jun Wei sarcastically.

"That was unfortunate, but not what I meant" said the Professor coldly.

"The assimilation of inorganic material into biological structures is not something we had witnessed before or could anticipate."

"So, what does this mean for your little science experiment?" said Jun Wei with concern, his mind racing, trying to think of what he was going to report to his father.

"Given the fact that the animal has regenerated using inorganic material, the possibility of repeat organ harvests is zero" said the Professor, "however I think there is more to learn if we just..."

Jun Wei cut him off, "my father isn't interested in what you might learn, he's interested in money."

"We have a lot of clients back home who want a steady supply of organs. So as far as I can tell, these animals are failures."

Jun Wei needed to regain control of this situation, to prove to himself that he was capable of the trust his father had placed in him.

"I want you to put a bullet in their heads and get to work with fresh subjects" Jun Wei commanded.

"My father will be getting a full report on your incompetence Professor!"

"Listen to me...Sir..." said the Professor, apparently about to say something derogatory towards the younger man but thinking better of it.

"We need time to examine the subjects, and evaluate..."

"Are you openly disobeying me Professor?" said Jun Wei assertively.

"Just get one of your armed goons to do it" he spat.

"I don't think bullets would kill them at this point" the Professor responded dryly.

"Well find a way! We're in a goddamn volcano, just dump them outside. I want those things destroyed!" Jun Wei shouted as he stormed out of the boardroom.

Jun Wei had asked to be shown his assigned quarters so he could try and think of a way to explain the situation to his father.

His father was not a man who took setbacks well, especially after Jun Wei had impressed upon him that things would go smoothly under his supervision.

Too many rivals and sycophants hanging around the old man, all waiting for their chance to shine. Blood ties meant nothing in the corporate world, businessmen were just as savage a beast as the one he witnessed an hour ago.

He shuddered at the memory as a soft knock at the door grabbed his attention.

A pretty, young admin clerk stood at attention. "They are ready for you Sir" she said, as she gestured him to follow.

They walked down another long and claustrophobic corridor in silence. Jun Wei was not in the mood for small talk anyway.

They walked through a door at the end of the corridor which opened into a large empty room. The walls were more industrial in appearance compared to the clean, clinical laboratories he had seen so far.

In the middle of the room, the three large holding pens containing the bears had been placed. The occupants were all agitated by the disruption caused by their relocation.

The Grizzly bear, fur still caked in blood, pawed at the glass wall of its cell.

Technicians finished securing the cells and retreated to a nearby control room. The young clerk wordlessly ushered Jun Wei towards the same room, before turning and leaving through the door they had just come through.

Jun Wei walked cautiously across the room, keeping his eye on the cells just in case. He stepped through the door to see the two technicians, along with the Professor and other key medical personnel.

The Professor stared at him with a simmering anger in his eyes but said nothing. No doubt still licking his wounds from Jun Wei's verbal beat down earlier.

The door to the control room slid close and clicked shut with a hiss.

Jun Wei walked over to a large glass window looking back into the large room he was just in.

It dawned on him what he was looking at. This room was some sort of large waste disposal facility, an incinerator perhaps, he thought to himself.

"We are secure now, you may proceed", the Professor said to the two technicians.

The technicians readied themselves at a nearby control panel and started flicking switches and pushing buttons. A series of loud cracks came from the cells in the room, like restraints popping open.

Sure enough, the doors of the cells creaked open. The bears seized their chance for escape and pushed the doors fully open and strolled out into the larger room.

The Grizzly immediately saw them all through the glass and charged.

Jun Wei started to back up nervously, but the Professor stood his ground, somewhat pleased at Jun Wei's distress.

"We are perfectly safe in here. There is no way to get through the security glass" he said.

The Grizzly threw its weight at the glass, and harmlessly slid down, its claws unable to make even the tiniest scratch. The Bear growled and bit aimlessly at the glass, a hatred in its eyes Jun Wei had never seen before, apart from maybe the Professor a few moments ago.

At this point the other two bears had made their way over to investigate.

One of the technicians flipped a few switches, and the bears flinched at the loud whirring noise as three large cranes descended from the roof, clamped down on the now vacant cells, and hoisted them back up to the ceiling.

The Kodiak bear and the Black bear had started to investigate the room, looking for a way out, as the Grizzly continued to glare at them through the glass.

The Professor nodded at the expectant technicians wordlessly, who both proceeded to insert keys into slots on their respective control panels.

"3...2...1..." one of them said as they turned their keys in unison.

The main room came alive with flashing lights and blaring sirens. The bears ran aimlessly, spooked by the commotion.

Suddenly a split down the middle of the floor opened, as the two halves of the floor started to retract.

An orange glow emanated from the increasing hole in the floor. The air above it shimmered with the heat of the lava flow beneath it.

The bears moved away from the widening hole and towards the glass window of the control room. All three of the bears started pawing frantically at the window, no longer out for blood, merely looking for escape.

Soon the whole room was bathed in a glow as the air seemed to take on a life of its own. The bears let out agonising roars, as their fur first began to singe, then catch alight.

The floor continued to open at a slow and steady pace. The process seemed unusually cruel and drawn out to Jun Wei.

"This was never designed for live subject disposal. Only the removal of waste," said the Professor, sensing Jun Wei's discomfort.

"Cruel as it may seem, it is the only form of disposal we could think of to thoroughly eliminate the subjects...as per your wishes...Sir" he continued.

The bears soon stopped growling, and started making pained squeals, as their hair burnt off and their skin cooked from the heat in the room. The room was now a giant oven.

Jun Wei stared blankly at the bears as they panted in the heat and gasped for air as volcanic gases filled the room.

As the floor completed its final movement and fully retracted, Jun Wei found himself staring the largest of the three bears directly in the eyes, its eyes filled with hate and pain, as one by one their charred bodies toppled over the edge and into the waiting inferno.

CHAPTER 3

The bodies of the bears impacted with the lava flow deep below the facility, their bodies slowly being enveloped by the magma.

Deep within the burnt husks of the animals, a flurry of activity was occurring.

The millions of tiny nanomachines circulating through the tissues of the bears, continued to compensate for the harsh environment of the volcano. The sensory overload from burnt nerve cells pushed the machines to their limits.

The machines evaluated the situation and drew new conclusions as they got to work. Designed to work in even the most unhospitable of environments, the nanomachines carried out their primary function, to preserve life, no matter what.

The nanomachines leeched out of the bodies of the animals in search of building materials. The magma provided a rich source of minerals.

The tiny machines constructed new cells, new structures, new organs. Designing a new type of organism capable of survival in the inferno.

Soon the charred remains of the three animals started to transform. Body parts destroyed by the intense heat reformed, their structure reflecting the harsh environment they found themselves in.

Claws of rock, and molten flesh formed, as the animals stirred and dragged themselves through the hellscape.

Nightmarish claws of fire and brimstone grabbed hold of the large metal tubes that jutted out of the lava flow and ascended towards the facility suspended way above.

The primary heat exchanger that provided geothermal power to the facility would also serve to provide entry to the bears as they made the climb towards revenge.

Jun Wei slept fitfully, fatigued by the events of the long day.

In his dreams, he was face to face with the bears with only a large pane of glass between them. But this time, he was in the waste disposal room, while the bears observed him from the safety of the control room.

The bears appeared to be engrossed in the information on the displays in front of them, as one of them pushed a lever with a massive paw.

Jun Wei spun around as he saw the floor start to move. The orange glow filling the room as he could feel the heat burn his skin.

He tried to scream but nothing came out. The skin on his hands bubbled as his clothes burst into flames. Still no screams came out, as the widening hole in the floor crept closer towards him. He turned back towards the observing bears, now wearing lab coats and taking notes excitedly on oversized clipboards. The sight was as horrifying as it was amusing to him, as he tumbled backwards to his doom.

Jun Wei woke with a jolt, a sense of confusion gripping him as he shook off the nightmare and remembered where he was. The previously dark room was illuminated by a strobing red light on the roof. The colour of the light momentarily flashed him back to the terrible glow from his nightmare.

Jun Wei pulled on his clothes and stared at the intercom next to his bed, trying to figure out how it worked and who he could ask what was going on.

At that moment, his door opened, and an armed security guard stepped in. "Sir, I need you to come with me right now" said the guard, as he ushered Jun Wei out the door and down the hallway.

As they walked down the long corridor towards the main laboratory complex, Jun Wei tried to wrap his head around what was going on.

Obviously, some sort of alarm had been triggered judging by the light in his room, yet no alarm sirens could be heard. Nobody else seemed to be hurrying about as if there was an emergency, and why was the guard armed? *Why not send the pretty little admin clerk to collect him* he thought? That would have at least been a welcome sight after such a horrible dream.

They entered the main laboratory, and Jun Wei saw the Professor along with several members of the security team staring intently at some monitors.

"There has been a breach" said the Professor cautiously.

"We are not sure of the details yet, but it appears to have come from the primary heat exchanger" he continued, "we chose to trip the silent alarm to alert you to the situation without bringing the whole facility into it."

A large Caucasian man with a short greying crew cut, decked out in full military combat fatigues, looked up from the monitor he was staring at intensely.

"This is our chief of security, Major Svenning," said the Professor.

Jun Wei recognised the man from the security team that subdued the rampaging grizzly bear. He had been the one that wanted to put a bullet in the creature's head then and there.

The Major turned away slightly and placed his hand to his earpiece, as if he were listening in on another conversation.

"My men are in position" he said in a gruff tone.

"It might not be anything" said the Professor, "but the heat exchanger does provide a certain level of vulnerability and a way into the facility that is unsecure."

"It was considered an acceptable risk, as the only way to access it is from the underside of the facility. The harsh environment and intense heat would be enough of a deterrent for any potential assault force."

"But still, it's a risk" interjected the Major, "which is why we have sensors in that area to detect any unauthorised movement" he continued. "And we were just informed there is a lot of unauthorised movement."

The Major pushed a few buttons on a nearby console, and the main display screen in the room flicked over to display what appeared to be head mounted camera feeds from several security personnel.

"Proceed with caution Alpha team" said the Major.

"Roger that" crackled a response over the radio.

Jun Wei watched as the team made their way along the corridors in the bowels of the facility.

The view from the camera feed was hard to make out, the corridors were dark, and the only illumination was from similar silent alarm lights to that he had seen in his room.

"Switching to night vision" came a voice over the radio, and the camera feeds switched to a ghostly green colour.

As the soldiers inched down the corridors, checking blind spots and communicating with an array of hand signals, Jun Wei could feel a sense of dread creeping up his spine.

As the soldier on point rounded the corner of the narrow access corridor, he seemed to blurt out an involuntary "...what the hell?" as the rest of his team fell in behind him.

Jun Wei was unsure of what he was seeing from the green tinted footage. At the end of the hallway the soldiers were staring down, there seemed to be a large rock formation blocking the far end.

As the soldiers made their way towards the formation, someone let out a gasp as the rocks shifted and moved. A low growl cut across the intercom, hollow and metallic.

Then the firing began.

Machine gun fire rang out from the radio in a tinny explosion. The screens went white as the muzzle flash from the weapons overloaded the sensors of the night vison cameras. Yells and commands could be heard underneath the din, as the Major shouted commands to his squad leader.

Yells turned into screams, the laboratory echoed with the sounds of gunfire and metallic grunts and growls. It was impossible to see what was happening on screen, with every camera feed strobing with muzzle flashes.

One of the soldiers broke off the firefight and retreated, his camera feed clearing up as he moved double time down the industrial corridors. All the other displays were now quiet, either displaying nothing but black or static.

The gun fire had stopped as abruptly as it had started, the only noise now being the laboured breaths of the last remaining soldier as he frantically ran though the labyrinth of corridors.

The soldier was in pitch darkness now, but the feed from his night vision was clear. He looked down a long corridor, and a light started to appear from around the corner. The light increased in intensity as the source rounded the corner and stepped into view.

In the contrast of the dark corridor, the silhouette of the bear was unmistakable. Its body glowed a fierce white in the green of the night vision.

The last remaining soldier's screams over the radio echoed through the laboratory as his camera feed turned to static. Everyone in the room stared blankly, trying to process what they had just seen.

The Major spoke up first, "Bravo team to position" he barked into his radio. A blaring siren cut across the room, as emergency lights started flashing.

"Sensors have detected a large spike of heat moving from the heat exchange to the main complex" said the Professor, "but it isn't outside heat getting in, it's happening within the facility".

The whole facility was on alert now, all staff had been roused from their sleep and were working frantically to control the situation.

The Major was gearing up with a small group to back up Bravo team, as the Professor monitored the facilities systems and directed staff to try and identify what they were up against.

Jun Wei tried his best to stay out of the way.

"We destroyed those bears, we watched them fall into the lava…" Jun Wei said quietly over the Professor's shoulder.

"We don't know what we saw, there was a lot of interference…" the Professor responded.

"We don't know what we saw..." he repeated, sounding less convinced.

"We have seen what those things can do, and we know at this point they are becoming unstoppable", Jun Wei said forcefully.

"I think at this point I need to leave," he said to no one in particular as he backed away towards the exit.

Jun Wei stared at the signs stencilled on the walls pointing the direction to the various wings of the facility, trying to think where his pilot might be, when he spied the young admin clerk from earlier.

She jumped as he grabbed her arm. She looked panicked and confused.

"I need to find my pilot" he said to her. She stared bewildered, then slowly nodded.

Together they walked down another long hallway. They were all starting to look the same to Jun Wei, so he was grateful for the guide.

People moved hurriedly in the opposite direction, paying no attention to them.

The lights in the hallway dimmed and flickered briefly. Jun Wei could hear a rhythmic popping sound not too far away. It took him a moment, but he recognised the sound as automatic weapons fire.

As they quickened their pace, the machine gun fire started to get louder, and soon that noise was joined by shouts and screams.

The wall of the corridor in front of them burst open with a screech.

Jun Wei and the clerk skidded to a halt as a wave of hot air hit them. A large hot blob had smashed through the wall and oozed slowly in their direction.

The blob looked like molten lava, as it glowed red hot, but it did not move like how Jun Wei would have expected. It moved with purpose, like it knew they were there and was seeking them out.

Backing away, the pair watched transfixed the blob changing shape as it moved down the hallway towards them.

Two elongated trunks stretched out from the front of the blob, the tips taking form in the shape of massive paws. The paws pushed down against the floor, heaving the blob up off the ground. Another protrusion emerged and from it, and a massive head formed.

The blob took on more of a bear shape with each step, but it retained the texture of molten rock.

The bear snarled at Jun Wei, with literal fire burning in its eyes. The look was unmistakable, it was the Kodiak bear. Jun Wei had seen that same look before it at fallen to its supposed death.

Fear gripped Jun Wei as he could only make long staggered steps backwards, eyes locked on the creature, mind racing.

The bear started to charge, but as it lurched forwards, its hind legs lost form and sagged back into a molten blob.

Maintaining its form seemed to take a lot of concentration, so it dragged itself forward on its front legs at a steady pace, the bulk of its body oozing behind it.

The young clerk hid behind Jun Wei as they retreated, making unintelligible noises and sobs.

As they backed down the corridor, it intersected with another. Jun Wei did not even see the panic-stricken researcher running down the other passage before they collided.

Jun Wei sat up dazed, his ears ringing.

Whoever had crashed into them, had already fled without even checking to see if they were ok.

A shrill scream overcame the ringing. Jun Wei spun around on the floor to see the clerk also on the ground, reaching out to him, her leg in the grasp of one of the Kodiak's massive paws.

The clerk screamed and thrashed in the Kodiak's grip, her flesh searing, and her clothes starting to burn.

The Kodiak oozed its massive bulk towards its trapped prey. Jun Wei skidded his feet against the floor, trying to regain his footing and stand up again, the soft leather soles of his designer shoes found no grip on the smooth floor.

Jun Wei could only scoot backward, terror gripping him, as he watched the molten blob of the bear slowly envelope the clerk, feet first, as she shifted between cries of pain and screams of terror.

The Kodiak reached out towards him with a glowing, red-hot claw, when a loud gunshot rang overhead.

The point-blank blast from the high calibre handgun, split the bear's head open, as it recoiled from the shot with a grunt.

Strong arms hoisted Jun Wei to his feet, as he saw the Major empty his clip into the creature.

Two of the Major's men flanked Jun Wei, weapons at the ready, as the four of them retreated down the hallway and away from the oozing Kodiak.

At another junction, the two soldiers took up defensive positions, covering two different directions, as the Major spoke into his radio. "We have him, we are coming to you" he said.

The Major tapped the soldiers on the shoulder and wordlessly they covered the rear as the group made their way through the corridors towards the central lab.

As they reached the end of the corridor, Jun Wei could see that a big heavy bulkhead door had been lowered.

Jun Wei could see the Professor on the other side through the door's small porthole.

"One moment" he said,

"I'll release the locks".

A thunderous noise from behind spun Jun Wei away from the door. Heavy footsteps echoed against the metallic walls of the corridor. The two soldiers opened fire as soon as the creature rounded the corner.

The bullets pinged against hard stone, sending chips flying. The bear stood at the end of the corridor and let out a low rumble.

Judging by its size, Jun Wei surmised this was the Black bear. Unlike the red-hot magma form of the Kodiak, the Black bear looked like it had been roughly chiselled out of black volcanic rock.

It growled another low echoing grunt as it charged, stone feet clanging against the metal floor with each step.

The noise was unbelievably loud in the confines of the corridor, between the machine gun fire and the charging bear, gunfire ricocheting off its tough exterior.

The bulkhead door hissed behind Jun Wei and slowly started to retract upwards. Another few seconds and the bear would be on them. Jun Wei dropped to his stomach and wormed his way under the door. The Professor grabbed his arm and pulled him through.

A moment later, the Major leopard crawled under the gap, joining them on the other side.

The Major jumped to his feet and through the porthole of the slowly rising bulkhead door, saw that the Black bear had nearly reached his men.

Without a word, the Major reached out and grabbed a small emergency lever next to the door.

The door hissed again and dropped shut with a heavy thud. The two men on the other side barely could register their surprise when the black bear slammed into them, crushing them against the bulkhead door.

"They wouldn't have made it" the Major said coldly.

As he turned away, the Black bear thudded against the heavy door in a futile attempt to get in.

"The facility is heavily compromised" said the Major as he studied a large bank of displays, all flashing various alerts and warnings.

"Most of my men are dead. There is no chance for containment at this point."

"We must awaken *the dragon* then..." said the Professor quietly.

The two men stared at each other in silence at the utterance, before Jun Wei broke the tension.

"What the hell does that mean? We have enough going on here without dragons getting involved" he spat.

"We need to get to my helicopter and get out of here."

The Professor held up a hand and gestured for calm.

"The dragon is a failsafe measure, to be used in the event of a full facility breach."

"Under no circumstances can the research of this facility be allowed to fall into our rival's hands, or to be made public."

"It's a self-destruct mechanism" the Major said bluntly.

"A small tactical nuke, enough to completely destroy the facility, but low yield enough to be confined to the volcano."

"As far as anyone will know, it will be chalked up to volcanic activity."

The Major walked over to a nearby computer terminal and entered in a code.

A narrow pedestal rose from the floor near the centre of the room. The pedestal had a variety of switches and buttons on it, as well as a large numerical keypad next to a LED display panel.

"The three of us should be sufficient authorisation" said the Professor, as he keyed a sequence into the keypad.

The Professor took off his glasses and placed his eye in front of a retinal scanner. A second later, a green light pinged on and the Professor took a step back.

The Major placed his eye in front of the scanner, and a second green light pinged into existence. The Major stepped back and motioned Jun Wei towards the pedestal.

A red flash momentarily blinded Jun Wei as he stared into the scanner. A second later, a third light joined the others. The LED display next to the keypad lit up and started counting backwards.

They had 20 minutes.

The Major checked his weapon as he peaked out of the small window on the closed bulkhead door. They were going to have to pass back through the locked door they entered through, in order to backtrack towards the facilities helipad.

Jun Wei had been concerned with the fate of his pilot, until Major Svenning assured him he could operate the helicopter.

A calm, digitised voice rang out over the facilities PA system. "*Dragon protocol active, you have 19 minutes to reach minimum safe distance.*"

The Major finished his sweep, the coast seemed clear.

The Black bear had wandered off, once it realised it couldn't breach the heavy door.

The door hissed and once again slowly started to lift, as the Major pulled the release handle.

Hot bile ran up his throat and into Jun Wei's nose, as he struggled not to vomit at the sight on the other side of the door.

The two trapped soldiers, or what was left of them, was smeared all over the corridor, like they had fallen into an industrial meat grinder.

The three men tiptoed through the gore and down the corridor. The narrow space made it impossible to see what was around the corner until it was too late.

The Major lead the way, pistol drawn. *As if bullets would do much,* Jun Wei thought to himself.

They made their way through the maze of corridors, past the burnt and maimed remains of the staff who once worked there so proudly. It was impossible to tell who these people were anymore, but the looks of fear etched on their corpses was evident.

"*You now have 10 minutes to reach minimum safe distance*" the calm robotic voice announced.

After so many lookalike corridors, Jun Wei recognised they were in the hallway where he was first greeted by the Professor when they arrived.

The airlock to the helipad was just up ahead. It would be cutting it close, but they would make it.

From memory, Jun Wei recalled a hatch, like a door on a submarine, followed by a set of steps that led up to a clean room where they stored the protective gear needed to make the hazardous trip outside the facility and to the helipad.

Sudden movement ahead caught Jun Wei's eye, and he froze.

It took a moment to register the figure near the hatch. It was his pilot.

As they approached, Jun Wei could see the burns across the man's arms and face, the wild, panicked look in his eyes.

The Pilot locked eyes with him for a moment, before he grabbed hold of the heavy hatch and started to push it close behind him.

Jun Wei let out a yell, telling the pilot to stop and wait, but he continued to strain and push the hatch.

"He's going to lock us in here" said the Major as he broke into a sprint towards the hatch.

As he ran, the Major levelled his pistol and fired. Heavy shots impacted against the steel hatch, the noise reverberated down the corridor like a canon had gone off.

The Major threw his body weight against the hatch just before it closed. He pushed hard against it, stopping it from fully closing and locking, as Jun Wei and the Professor ran towards him to help.

As the three of them pushed against the heavy hatch, and the Pilot who was pushing with all his strength to close it, a low metallic growl reverberated down the hallway towards them.

Jun Wei spun and put his back against the hatch, pushing with his legs, his shoes slipping against the floor.

At the end of the hallway, a hulking beast stalked towards them. The Grizzly bear strode down the hallway almost casually, like it was savouring the moment.

Its body was made up of segments of black rock, like armour plating, but underneath that, its body glowed red hot. It was like seeing the molten core of the Earth itself come to life. Tectonic plates shifting and moving with each step.

Soon it was joined by the Kodiak and the Black bear. The three bears made their way towards the three men, as a wave of heat preceded them.

The Pilot on the other side of the hatch heard their growls, and pressed his face to glass porthole of the hatch. His face contorted in fear, and a newfound flood of adrenalin gave him the strength he needed.

Despite the three-to-one odds, the Pilot was winning this contest of strength. The door was nearly closed, only a small gap was stopping it from clamping shut.

The Major looked at the Pilots face, pushed against the porthole, transfixed with fear, and made his move. He placed the tip of his pistol against the glass and pulled the trigger.

Chips of glass sprayed everywhere, and a red mist painted the wall. The hatch swung open against the weight of the three men, as the Pilot's body slumped back against the stairs.

Quickly filing through the hatch, the men pushed their collective weight back against the door as the Grizzly closed the gap. The hatch closed with a click, and locked.

The men backed away quickly and retreated a few steps up the staircase, as a large rocky snout pushed through the broken porthole with a grunt.

"Let's see you get through that!" shouted Jun Wei almost triumphantly.

The bear paused for a moment and let out another grunt, almost like an acknowledgment to the challenge.

The black stone of the bear's snout started to glow red, as waves of heat started to radiate from it.

The Grizzly pushed its now molten head against the small porthole, its form compressing and flowing through the gap.

Jun Wei watched in disbelief as the molten form squeezed through the small opening. The heat was becoming intense, causing him to back up the staircase.

The heat of the creature transferred to the hatch and the weight of the Grizzly's bulk squeezing through the porthole soon caused the metal to screech and buckle. It wouldn't be long before the hatch tore off its hinges like it was made of wet cardboard.

Nobody wanted to be around when it did, and the three men ran up the staircase to the clean room where the protective gear was stored.

Jun Wei thought back to how long it took him to get into the bulky protective gear when they first landed, ten minutes at least. There was no way they would get out in time if they needed to put all that gear on first.

The Major and the Professor seemed to have the exact same thought.

"We are going to have to make a run for the helicopter...unprotected," said the Professor.

"That's suicide!" protested Jun Wei, but what choice did they have? Run across the scorching, toxic hellscape to the waiting helicopter, or wait here and see what got them first, the bears or the explosion?

"Take these" said the Major, as he threw both the Professor and Jun Wei a small air tank with a face mask attached.

"It won't give you much, but it should be enough to get you to the helicopter without breathing the fumes" he said.

The Professor ripped open a nearby First Aid kit attached to the wall and fished out three small metallic squares.

Ripping off the plastic cover, the Professor shook the square until it unfurled into a large metal sheet, like tinfoil.

Jun Wei recognised it as the same type of emergency blankets used to treat people suffering from hypothermia.

"Wrap this tightly around you" said the Professor, "It should help reflect some of the heat energy."

"Or cook us like a roast chicken", said Jun Wei as he wrapped himself in the blanket regardless.

Metal screeches and growls rose up from the stairwell as the Major grabbed the release handle for the outer airlock.

The blast of heat was intense and immediate as the door swung open.

Jun Wei squinted as he could feel his eyes drying out in the heat. His breathing caught in his chest as the men ran out of the airlock and towards the waiting helicopter.

100 metres may well have been 100 kilometres in this heat.

Jun Wei's heart hammered as he rushed towards the helicopter, still thankfully where he had left it.

Piling into the cramped airlock of the helicopter, the door slid shut behind them and they were immediately greeted by a blast of cool air as the aircraft sealed itself tight.

Jun Wei stripped off the space blanket and tossed aside his air supply. The skin on his hands was already red and starting to blister. He ran to the bar and grabbed a bottle of water from a small refrigerator.

His eyes and throat stung, but the cool water was refreshing, as he poured the remainder of the bottle over his head.

He passed another bottle to the Professor who accepted it eagerly.

The Major ran past him and jumped into the pilot's seat, initiating the start-up sequence.

The engines sprang to life, the soft hum barely audible from inside the aircraft, as the helicopter slowly started to lift off from the platform.

Jun Wei looked out the window, back towards the facility and let out a scream.

The helicopter rocked violently as the Black bear slammed into the side of it.

The Major over-corrected for the impact and the helicopter drifted back towards the facility.

All it would take was for their rotor to clip something and it would be all over for them.

Jun Wei looked out the window at the Black bear, clinging to one of the pods that housed the landing gear.

The Major adjusted the helicopter and straightened out, once again lifting away from the platform, as a flaming bear paw scratched at the window.

The Kodiak had now joined in and had attached itself to the side of the helicopter, its molten body gripping the aircraft's fuselage.

Fortunately, the helicopter was designed to work in such harsh environments, so the bear's heat did very little damage as their claws swiped ineffectively at the reinforced windows.

The helicopter also served as the primary method for transporting cargo to and from the facility, so the additional weight did little to slow their ascent once the Major had compensated for it.

The facility dropped away as the helicopter rapidly rose towards the lip of the volcano, its extra passengers could do nothing more but hold on at this point.

Another few moments they would be clear of the lip and of the imminent blast.

Still staring out the window at the stowaways, Jun Wei looked down towards the landing platform and saw the Grizzly standing there, its body starting to emanate a bright orange glow.

The Grizzly let out a sudden blast, an explosion released from its body, hurling it skywards like a missile.

Jun Wei shouted out a warning, but it was too late for evasive action in such a narrow space.

The helicopter cleared the lip of the volcano and sored into the night sky as the Grizzly impacted with it mid-air.

The tail of the helicopter disintegrated with the impact, and the helicopter went into a death spiral.

Alarms blared, and as Jun Wei held on for dear life, he watched as the Bears still clinging to the side were flung off by the rapid spinning of the helicopter and into the forest below.

The Major cut power to the engines to attempt an autorotation manoeuvre and bring the helicopter under some sort of control.

The spinning stopped but they were still falling rapidly, the damage too severe to compensate for.

There was nothing to do at this point except brace for impact.

Deep in the volcano, in the eery quiet of the facility populated now only by the corpses of its former staff, a calm robotic voice addressed nobody.

'Dragon protocol active in 3...2...1...have a nice day.'

CHAPTER 4

The echoing roar of the blast rumbled through the forest.

Clayton Wallace slammed the brakes on his jeep and slid to a halt. The music that had been blasting through his stereo had been loud, but not loud enough to drown out the noise still faintly echoing.

Clayton climbed out of the vehicle, stubbed out his freshly lit joint on his boot and listened. The night was eerily quiet.

The forest was usually quiet, but there was always some owl softly hooting, or small animal scurrying through the undergrowth. It seemed like everything had stopped to listen and figure out the source of the noise.

Slowly crickets started to chirp, and the background noise of the forest came back to life. Clayton shook his head and climbed back into his jeep.

Being a forest ranger was a pretty easy job, as far as Clayton was concerned. His father had insisted on him getting a job and getting out of the house and had pulled a few strings to get him the position.

Clayton was mainly responsible for checking on the various camping sites that were dotted through the forests surrounding Lake Ursa.

He spent most of his time busting teenagers, not much younger than himself, looking to get drunk and high. More often than not he would join in.

He was unsure of what to do with massive explosion noises though. His mind immediately turned to Mount Arktos, but that volcano was supposed to be dormant, or so he had been told.

He didn't take his job too seriously. Learning about volcanoes and memorising sections of the Parks and Wildlife Code was not his idea of fun.

The only time he really paid attention to his supervisors was when there were reports of wildlife attacks. Clayton was not a big fan of any animal that could eat him, and there were plenty of mountain lions, wolves and bears out in the forest.

Fortunately, those kinds of things were rare, and he had never had any problems cruising around the backwoods.

The town of Lake Ursa had learnt to live in harmony with the wildlife native to the area. The lake and town having been named for the high density of bears in the area, way back in the pioneering days.

Clayton climbed back in his jeep and cranked the volume on his stereo once more as he drove through one of the forest's dark dirt roads.

Up ahead he could see the glow of a campfire. It wasn't near any of the forest's designated campgrounds.

Pulling over, he turned off the jeep and got out. Music and faint laughter floated through the air.

He knew all the little spots the teenagers of the town liked to hang out at, he had spent plenty of time there himself instead of focusing on school.

One of Clayton's favourite parts of the job was sneaking up and busting campers without permits.

Most of the time they would buy him off with booze or pot which suited him fine, it also meant he didn't have to fill in a report afterwards.

Creeping towards the campsite, he could hear the camper's voices. Two girls complained as three boys teased them and made crude jokes.

"I'm telling you, the town just got bombed. It's all gone, we're the last people left..." joked one of the boys.

"Yeah, what if it's World War Three, and we need to repopulate the world..." said another.

"Well, the human race is going to die out then", said one of the girls sarcastically.

Clayton recognised one of the boys, Tyler Munroe the school's quarterback. He was tall and athletic with short cropped blond hair and a constant smirk, as if he was just as impressed with himself as everyone else seemed to be.

It was time to have a little fun, Clayton thought to himself.

"What's going on here?" shouted Clayton in a booming voice, stepping into the light of the campfire as the girls screamed in surprise.

One of the other boys reached for a nearby compound bow that was resting on his backpack, before thinking better of the idea.

"You kids are in deep trouble, for violating *camping code...uh...69...*" said Clayton in his deepest and most authoritative voice, before bursting out into laughter.

"Clayton!" shouted Tyler, "You scared the crap out of me, man."

The campers looked on as Clayton walked up and gave their friend an elaborate handshake.

"What's happening, Tyler?" said Clayton, "Who are your friends?"

Tyler took a swig from a can of beer, as he reached into a nearby cooler for another, handing it to Clayton.

"That's Bobby, and his girlfriend Kayla" he said as he pointed to a couple cozied up together in front of the fire.

"That's Aisha" he said pointing to the other girl, who smiled shyly.

"And that's Adam. Be very quiet....*he's huntin' wabbits*" he said in a bad Elmer Fudd voice, gesturing to the boy with the bow as the rest of the group laughed.

Clayton had been a few years ahead of Tyler in school but knew him from the local country club, as their fathers golfed together.

Tyler's dad used to be some sort of big-shot attorney from Charleston until he decided to drop out of the rat race and move his family out to the peace and quiet of Lake Ursa.

He was just another one of the town's rich kids, except unlike Clayton, Tyler's father actually gave him money, as evident by the shiny new pickup truck parked nearby.

Clayton liked him well enough. He had busted him a number of times out in the woods with friends, trying to impress whatever girl he was currently pursuing. He always had plenty of beer to share and good weed.

"So, man what was that loud boom just before?" Tyler asked.

"Bobby thinks the Russians have started dropping bombs" he laughed.

"Not sure dude, that's above my paygrade" said Clayton with a laugh as he sparked up another joint and passed it around the group.

Tyler sat down next to Aisha and casually put his arm around her, as he offered her one of his beers. She smiled and quickly averted her gaze as she caught Clayton's eye.

She seemed way too classy for Tyler, Clayton thought to himself.

"Do you think it could be the volcano?" She said timidly.

"We were studying it in science class. We were told it was dormant."

"No idea," said Clayton.

"My job is making sure people like Tyler don't leave too many beer cans lying around the forest."

"Well, I better help you earn that pay cheque then" said Tyler as he crumpled his empty beer can against his forehead and threw it over his shoulder with a laugh.

Aisha peeled Tyler's arm off her shoulder and stood up, looking towards the black silhouette of the mountain in the moonlit sky.

"My dad says there is some volcanologist guy that keeps bugging him", said Clayton.

"Maybe there is something going on we don't know?" he said with a shrug.

"Aren't *Vulcanologists* the guys with the pointy ears..." Kayla suddenly butted in.

The group groaned and laughed as she looked around, genuinely confused.

"No sweety", said Aisha, "You're thinking of the TV show..."

Aisha stopped abruptly as a low rumbling growl wound its way through the trees.

"What was that?" hissed Kayla, alarmed.

After sitting there quietly the whole time, Adam suddenly jumped to his feet at the noise.

Bow in hand, he detached an arrow from the quiver attached to the side of his bow and quickly nocked it.

"It's coming from down the hill, could be a bear?" he said excitedly, already starting towards the direction of the sound.

"Leave it alone" shouted Tyler after him, as he got to his feet.

"I'm telling you; you're not going to bag anything out here, especially not a bear."

Clayton felt a surge of panic.

Camping without a permit was one thing but hunting without one was something entirely different. If this guy kills something, they all could be in big trouble.

Clayton dropped his beer and ran after Tyler and Adam.

Bobby got up and started walking after them as well. The girls not wanting to be left alone, soon followed.

Making his way down the hill in the dark was proving to be difficult.

Clayton wished he had remembered to bring the torch stored in the jeep. The campfire had ruined his night vision, but fortunately there was enough moonlight to avoid tripping on fallen logs and tumbling down the hill.

After stumbling through the forest for several minutes, Clayton caught up to Tyler and Adam at the bottom of the hill. They were staring intently into a nearby clearing.

"Hey man, I can't have you hunting stuff out here" Clayton said.

Adam held up his hand to cut him off and pointed at the clearing up ahead.

"Over there, past those trees..." said Adam.

Clayton blinked a few times, trying to get his eyes to adjust faster in the low light. Adam seemed to be pointing to a large rock in the clearing.

The three of them stood silently, trying to make out the shape in the moonlight as the others came crashing through the trees behind them.

The rock seemed to move at the noise, and the same low rumbling growl came from its direction, much louder this time.

"Shhh..." Adam hissed.

"I'm trying to figure out what that is" he said.

Kayla reached into her pocket, and soon they were all blinded as she turned the light of her smartphone on.

Clayton groaned as his night vision was destroyed once again.

"Shine it over there" he said, pointing at the rock and away from his eyes.

Adam stalked forward, bow ready, towards the strange rock. It looked jet black, even with the light shining on it. He could feel warmth radiating off it as he reached out to touch it.

"Maybe it's a meteorite, that would explain the boom..." He called back to the rest of the group.

The rock moved suddenly towards him, and something sharp raked across his thigh.

He let out a shout as he fell backwards.

His pants felt wet, and in the light from the phone, he could see a large red gash rapidly filling with blood opening up.

The rock let out another loud metallic growl, and moved violently, as if trying to free itself from the ground it seemed to be embedded in.

With one last pull, the creature freed itself.

The Black bear turned towards the group and stood up on its hind legs. The girls screamed as the bear let out a long guttural roar.

The bear's roar was soon echoed by a deeper, more booming growl.

On the far side of the clearing, Clayton could see an orange glow through the thick trees, almost as if cast by someone holding a flaming torch.

Branches snapped and trees shook, as the glow made its way towards the clearing, a hollow metallic grunting getting louder all the while.

Pine needles that littered the forest floor burst into flames with each footstep of the creature.

The Kodiak reached the edge of the clearing and squeezed through a tight gap between two large trees. Its form contracted and expanded as it made its body fit through the narrow space.

The bark of the trees ignited as it came in contact with the bear's red-hot molten body. The creatures body glowed brightly as it flowed through the gap into the clearing.

The clearing was soon illuminated by the glow of the Kodiak as it reformed back into the shape of a bear, and slowly made its way towards the group.

Bobby and Tyler rushed over and helped Adam to his feet.

With a pained and panicked expression on his face, which to Clayton looked like he was going into shock, Adam nocked an arrow.

The Black Bear now having freed itself from the soft earth it seemed to have been partially embedded in, started to advance towards them.

Adam drew back his bow and released, the Black Bear only a few meters away.

The arrow hit the bear squarely in the head and bounced harmlessly off the creature's rocky hide.

Tyler and Bobby darted backward away from the creature as it lunged forward. Its paw swatting down their friend, who could not limp out of the way fast enough.

The Black bear bit down hard, clamping its jaw around the fallen teenager's groin and inner thigh. Adam screamed at the others to help as the Black bear tossed him effortlessly towards the approaching Kodiak bear.

Clayton stood there frozen in place as the events unfolded in slow motion.

The girls screamed at Bobby and Tyler to do something. Tyler looked at the girls, then Clayton, then towards Adam and the two bears.

Without a word, he took off at a sprint back up the hill toward their campsite.

Snapping out of his daze, Clayton looked at Bobby, who also seemed to be frozen with terror.

"Come on!" he shouted as he ran towards Adam who moaned and writhed on the ground in pain.

Spurred on by the command, Bobby ran to help his friend.

Bobby and Clayton each grabbed an arm and tried to drag Adam to his feet.

In the glow of the Kodiak, Clayton could see the damage the Black bear's bite had done. Adam would not be walking, and they would need to drag him to safety.

The Kodiak took slow and deliberate steps forward.

It seemed to be having trouble holding up its own weight, as parts of its body sagged and pooled on the ground. The heat coming from its body was overpowering, even from several feet away.

The Kodiak reared up and lashed out with a massive paw.

The swipe sprayed an arc of hot globs of its own molten body.

Clayton ducked the incoming fire, but Bobby who was fixated on his dying friend, acted too slowly.

The molten blobs impacted Bobby in the face and chest, clinging to him like napalm. He screamed, and instinctively tried to wipe away the burning slag.

His hands recoiled as they touched the red-hot lava, causing him to scream again. Soon his clothes ignited from the heat, as he turned into a human bonfire.

Clayton dropped Adam and fell backwards.

He watched in horror as Bobby flailed about, consumed by fire, and staggered blindly into the waiting jaws of the Kodiak.

In the intense glow of the fire, Clayton saw the Black bear charge. It moved a lot faster than its rocky form looked like it should.

He rolled to the side as it ran into the fray. Its heavy stone feet trampling Adam as he lay motionless on the ground.

Hands reached down and grabbed Clayton's arms.

The girls strained as they helped pull him to his feet.

"RUN!" he shouted, and the three of them sprinted up the hill back towards where the vehicles were parked at their camp.

The light from Kayla's phone bounced erratically as they ran, the shadows from the dense trees strobing as they struggled up the incline, hearts racing.

Behind them they could hear the Black Bear smashing through the trees in pursuit.

Fortunately, the forest was thick, and the trees tightly packed together. Clayton and the girls weaved their way through the trees as the pursuing Black Bear had to take a less direct route.

The three of them reached the top of the hill and back to camp. Tyler was standing there doubled over, trying to catch his breath.

He spun around, eyes wide with fear. The crashing noise grew louder as the Black bear charged up the hill.

Tyler darted across the camp towards his pickup truck.

The engine roared to life, as Clayton and the two girls ran towards the safety of the vehicle.

Just as they reached for the door handle, Tyler slammed down the gas pedal, and the truck lurched off with a spin of its wheels.

"Come back!" screamed Aisha, tears streaming down her face. The trio chased Tyler's truck out onto the long dirt road, shouting, trying to make him stop and wait.

Speeding away, Tyler looked back in the rear-view mirror as Clayton and the girls fell behind. He had to get away, away from those...*things!*

The truck sped along the long dark road. Up ahead in the distance, an object started to glow from a deep red to a bright orange.

The truck skidded to a halt, as Tyler flicked on the high beams.

The light from the truck illuminated the Grizzly as it stalked its way down the dirt road. The fissures across its stony body glowed fiercely, as it broke into a charge.

Tyler slammed down the gas pedal once more and revved the engine hard.

"No way this thing is getting in my way" he thought, as he put the truck into gear and raced towards the Grizzly.

Clayton and the girls watched in disbelief as Tyler played chicken with the charging bear.

The glow from the bear's body increased in intensity, before it discharged a blast from its body.

The Grizzly rocketed forward like a missile and smashed into the truck.

The front of the truck crumpled effortlessly with the impact, as the truck flipped onto its roof.

The Grizzly skidded to a halt along the dirt road, then quickly charged back towards the overturned vehicle.

The massive bear climbed on top of the smashed truck, the metal letting out a groan as it buckled under the weight.

The bear now glowed red hot all over, just like the larger bear they had seen in the clearing.

Fully illuminated by the bear's glow, Clayton could see Tyler pinned in the cab of the ruined truck, struggling to escape.

Clayton grabbed Aisha and Kayla's hands and pulled them through the forest running alongside the dirt road.

His jeep was parked further down the track. If they could just get to it and avoid running into the other bears lurking somewhere in the darkness, they might have a chance.

Tyler's shouts for help turned to panic, as the Grizzly's now molten body started to melt the body of the truck.

The upholstery inside the cab started to smoulder and catch alight. Clayton only had a moment to look back and catch Tyler's pleading stare, before the truck's fuel tank erupted, engulfing the truck in a fireball.

Up ahead in the moonlight, Clayton spotted the silhouette of his jeep. He fumbled for the keys, as he ushered the girls into the backseat.

After taking a quick breath to calm his nerves, he started the engine.

The Jeep roared to life, and he flicked on the headlights.

The Black bear lit up in front of the jeep, as it reared up and let out a deep growl. Its eyes glinted in the light, like two beads of onyx.

Clayton and the girls screamed in unison, as the Black bear slammed down on the hood of the jeep.

Clayton jammed the vehicle into reverse.

The bear's claws raked down the hood of the jeep as it backed up, leaving deep gashes in the metal. Clayton cranked the handbrake, and the jeep spun around 180 degrees.

The Black Bear gave chase, but soon lost interest as they sped away.

Clayton looked back at the creature in the rear-vision mirror, its cold black eyes reflecting in the moonlight.

They had to get back to town, people had to be warned.

CHAPTER 5

The night air was surprisingly cool for July, Professor Radford Hardcastle thought to himself as he stood on the front porch of his cabin.

The loud boom that had rung out earlier that night had woken him with a start. He had gotten dressed and put on a pot of coffee as he booted up his laptop and stepped outside into the night.

Hardcastle, a professor of volcanology, had moved to the small town of Lake Ursa only six months ago.

He had spent a long time in the world of academia, lecturing at universities all over the world. In recent years he had turned his attention to the detection and monitoring of previously unknown locations, high in potential volcanic activity.

It was time to move away from the safety of the classrooms and its speculative theories, to get out and start researching in the field.

To that end he had been drawn to the town of Lake Ursa and Mount Arktos.

Thought to be dormant, Mount Arktos was a draw card for the town, and dominated the landscape.

However, Hardcastle had his own theories about the level of activity inside the volcano, and the threat it could potentially have.

Mount Arktos had several curious traits that he had never seen in all his years of research.

At first glance, the mountain appeared to be a fairly standard stratovolcano, a large conical formation built up by many layers, with a steep profile and a summit crater.

It had reminded him of Mount Fuji in Japan, a mountain he had many fond memories of, and what had helped spark his interest in volcanoes at an early age.

Towards the base of the conical formation of the mountain, the structure of the mountain suddenly made an odd change and became a more gradual slope, a characteristic more commonly seen in shield volcanos like Mauna Loa on the island of Hawai'i.

It was effectively one volcano sitting on top of another type of volcano. Hardcastle had never seen such a bizarre structure before.

He surmised that Mount Arktos was a dormant supervolcano, much like Yellowstone National Park.

However, Yellowstone had erupted 640,000 years ago, causing any type of similar mountainous structure to collapse into a caldera.

Was he looking at a yet unerupted and unknown supervolcano type? An eruption from such a thing would have devastating environmental impacts on the entire country, and potentially the world.

This hypothesis was hotly contested in academic circles, and an air of mystique had sprung up around the volcano in recent years.

There seemed to be very little data being collected about the activity going on inside the mountain, and he was determined to find out why.

Six months ago, he had packed up everything and moved across the country to engage in his own research.

After establishing himself in a cosy little cabin in the woods, Hardcastle had tried to gain the appropriate approval from the local government to conduct his studies.

Frustratingly, the progress was slow. There were long waits for his requests to be even acknowledged, which were then denied without a reason being given.

It almost seemed that there was deliberate interference, stopping him from conducting his research.

If he was going to be denied his research through official channels, he would need to conduct some *unofficial* research.

Over the last few months, he had constructed his own seismic survey equipment and dotted them throughout the forests and areas around the mountain under the guise of collecting soil samples.

The local rangers had been more accommodating than the mayor's office in that regard, as long as he didn't venture too close to the mountain.

Hopefully his equipment could give some insight into the boom that had rocked him awake.

Hardcastle sipped his coffee and stared at the screen of his laptop, as the reports from his survey equipment slowly rolled in.

Signal strength was not that great up here in his cabin at the best of times but appeared to be worse than usual. Just another roadblock to his investigations it seemed.

Slowly the data downloaded and populated the screen. Hardcastle stared in disbelief and double checked what he was seeing. A massive spike of seismic activity had been recorded, and all his sensors confirmed it had originated from within the volcano itself.

He had never seen anything like this before. Normally volcanic activity tends to increase in intensity over time. It was highly unusual to see a massive jump in activity with no warning signs.

This was not something he could afford to wait on.

The town could be facing a profoundly serious eruption with little to no warning. The authorities needed to be alerted.

Hardcastle picked up his cell phone and went to dial when he noticed the phone was displaying zero bars.

"Just great..." he muttered.

Hardcastle packed up his laptop, jumped in his truck and headed to town. It was late but he hoped that someone would be in the mayor's office at this time of night.

Surely he was not the only person concerned by the deafening boom?

Hardcastle's cabin was on the outskirts of town, which he didn't exactly mind. The rent was cheaper and gave him some amazing views of the lake and mountain.

He tended to only go into town when he needed supplies, so hadn't really had much time to get to know the locals. He wasn't much of a people person despite lecturing so frequently. He had always enjoyed the solitude of nature.

But now, looking at the *'No Service'* message on his phone was making him regret living so far out in the sticks. Something was definitely off though, as he would usually have service by now.

As he got closer to town his cell service finally improved.

Hardcastle dialled the number for the mayor's office. He had called so many times over the last few months, trying to convince the mayor to grant him the licences and access he needed to do his research, that he had pretty much memorised the phone number by now.

He was in luck, the phone picked up almost straight away.

The line was crackly, but he recognised the voice of the mayor's executive assistant right away. She had denied him meetings with the mayor on more occasions than he could remember.

"Hello this is Professor Radford Hardcastle..." he began.

"The volcano guy, yes?" the assistant cut him off.

"Professor of Volcanology, yes..." he replied before being cut off again.

"Excellent" said the assistant, "The Mayor wants to talk to you immediately."

Hardcastle pulled his truck up at the front of the mayor's office. A large security guard and the mayor's assistant met him in the lobby and escorted him up to see the mayor.

Mayor Brenton Wallace was pacing his office as they walked in. This was the first time Hardcastle had met the man, despite months of persistence.

The mayor was in his mid-50's, only a few years older than Hardcastle himself, not that you would realise that by looking at the pair of them.

Hardcastle looked much younger than his age would have you believe. Apart from some greying around his temples and a bit of salt and pepper in his close-cropped beard, he still had a full head of black hair.

Hiking up mountains all over the world had kept him fit and strong over the years.

The mayor on the other hand, was grey and balding, no doubt exacerbated by his years in office, while he had the pudgy midsection of a man whose only exercise was the occasional round of golf.

Still, he definitely had a charismatic look to him and vaguely reminded Hardcastle of Barack Obama.

Hardcastle shook hands and proceeded to set up his laptop to show the mayor his findings.

The mayor, starting to pace the room again, seemed to have a different agenda for the meeting.

"Professor, we have a situation here" he began.

"Lake Ursa is a popular tourist destination in the summer. We get a lot of business here, especially over the fourth of July weekend."

"As you know, that is only a few days away and it's something our economy needs right now..."

Hardcastle turned away from his laptop to question this seemingly bizarre concern.

"Actually, Mr Mayor, given what I am about to show you, we should start thinking about cancelling any celebrations and warning tourists not to come."

"I think this whole town is in very real danger right now..." he continued.

Mayor Wallace waved his hand at the suggestion, "I can assure you Professor that is not the case. We have scientists here, the best really, who have said that there is no danger."

Hardcastle stared at the man curiously. He was unaware of any other scientists in the town.

"That unexplainable boom earlier tonight certainly gave a few people a start, didn't it Genevieve?" said the mayor, directing his attention towards his assistant, who nodded silently.

"We've been getting calls about it from all over the place, and we've let them know everything is just fine."

"But that might not be enough to allay people's fears you see" said the mayor, walking over and closing the screen of Hardcastle's laptop.

"You are a respected expert in your field, so it would go a long way if you were to publicly put these fears to rest."

Hardcastle bristled at the suggestion.

Whoever these *experts* feeding this information to the mayor were, he had certainly never encountered such disregard for public safety before.

"Mr Mayor, I can assure you there is a very real danger here. I have been conducting my own research these last few months, and have uncovered data..."

"Research you do not have the permits for" said the mayor in a stern tone, shutting Hardcastle down.

Hardcastle knew he had said too much and had now put himself in a compromised position.

The mayor's expression softened, and he flashed a smile that had no doubt won him many votes over the years.

"Look, I'm sure we can work something out here." said the mayor.

"If you were to help us advise the public that the town is safe and that celebrations are still going ahead, I'm sure we could approve some of those requests you have submitted."

Hardcastle stood in stunned silence.

Did this man really value the town's economic prosperity over the safety of its residents?

Before he could answer, the silence was broken by a commotion downstairs in the lobby.

Hardcastle could hear the assistant arguing with someone, followed by a shout from the security guard and footsteps running up the stairs towards the office.

The office door burst open, and a young man stood there panting, a haunted expression across his face.

"Clayton!" exclaimed the mayor.

"I am in the middle of a meeting!" he fumed.

"Dad..." the young man panted, trying to catch his breath.

"Something happened... in the forest" he gasped.

"Well, I certainly don't want to hear about it, go explain it to your supervisor if it is so important" the mayor snapped back.

Clayton just ignored him as he paced the room, like a young version of his father, an array of emotions crossing his face as he spoke.

"We thought it was a rock, but then it got hot... then the other thing came, and it was like some sort of...lava..." Clayton choked out.

The word *lava* jumped out at Hardcastle.

Could the volcano have already started to erupt? He thought to himself.

Maybe this young man could give him some more information, it was obvious the mayor was stonewalling him at this point.

"Why don't I have a chat with him?" said Hardcastle.

"Ignore him, this is just my son," said the mayor.

"He smokes too much pot and then has these little freak outs", said the mayor turning a shade of red. Hardcastle could not tell if was from embarrassment or anger.

"Well seeing lava doesn't sound like something you would see while high" said Hardcastle.

"Yeah see, this guy knows..." Clayton trailed off as he stared at Hardcastle.

"Radford Hardcastle, professor of volcanology..." said Hardcastle with a little wave.

"Volcano guy!" blurted Clayton.

At least someone knows me thought Hardcastle.

"Why don't I have a word with your son and find out what he really saw?" said Hardcastle.

"That way I'll be better informed when I tell the public that there is nothing to worry about."

This seemed to strike the right chord, the mayor returning to his normal colour.

"Yes, yes. That is good to hear, and afterwards I'm sure we can talk more about your research", said the mayor slipping back into charm mode.

Hardcastle packed up his laptop and gently lead Clayton out of the room, despite his protests. Once he realised that his father wasn't going to listen, he came along quietly.

Outside the Mayor's office, Clayton's jeep was parked haphazardly next to Hardcastle's truck. Hardcastle noticed the deep gouges in the hood of the vehicle.

"Get in and tell me everything" said Hardcastle as he started up his truck.

CHAPTER 6

"That's impossible" said Hardcastle as he sped along the road out of town.

"I'm just telling you what I saw, man" said Clayton, having relayed his experience to a highly sceptical Hardcastle.

The whole thing sounded fantastical to him, yet his mind flashed back to the deep gouges he saw on the hood of Clayton's truck. Something big had done that damage.

"Are you sure you saw what you saw?" he enquired.

"You think I just imagined the whole thing?" Clayton fired back, offended.

"I watched three people get torn apart by those things..." his voice suddenly getting quiet.

"I know how crazy it sounds," said Clayton.

"They were alive, they looked and acted like bears, but they were made from molten rock".

"You said there were two girls with you?" said Hardcastle.

"Maybe we could ask them to corroborate what you..."

"They were damn near catatonic by the time I dropped them of at the Sheriff's office" said Clayton angrily.

"They had just watched their friends die."

Clayton stared out the window as Hardcastle drove in silence, trying to piece together some sort of logical explanation.

Could there have been an ejection of lava from the volcano and these bears had been caught in it?

That would be implausible, thought Hardcastle. Lava flows can be hotter than 2200 degrees, more than enough to cook flesh, unless the animal's thick hides gave it a degree of protection. It would certainly explain why the animals were so enraged.

But something about the young man's story did not lend itself to that hypothesis.

He had claimed they had changed shape and moved in ways that would be impossible, especially for an animal suffering from deep burns.

Animal attacks were one thing, but the emergence of any type of volcanic material signalled a much great threat from the volcano itself.

The only way he would get answers would be to check out the scene himself, but he would need to take samples, and for that he would need to return home for equipment.

Hardcastle turned off the main roads and onto a dirt track, heading up into the mountains towards his cabin.

A short time later, they pulled up just outside of his cabin. Hardcastle stared for a moment and switched off the engine.

The lights were on inside. Had he forgotten to turn them off in his rush to get into town?

"Stay here, I'll be back when I've got my gear" he said.

Clayton nodded, he looked relieved to have a moment to himself to collect his thoughts.

Hardcastle walked up the wooden steps and pushed open his front door.

"I was wondering when you'd be back..." A woman's voice called out as he stepped through the door.

Hardcastle froze in disbelief as he saw the woman standing in his living room.

A flood of different emotions hit Hardcastle at the sight of the woman. It had been several years since Hardcastle had last seen her.

Her name was Meli Goodhams, or 'Honey' to her friends.

They had first met over a decade ago on the Hawaiian island of O'ahu. Honey had grown up there, her mother being a native islander, and her father, a military man stationed at Pearl Harbor military base.

Growing up she loved being active, be it surfing or hiking, as long as she was in nature.

An inquisitive mind, something she shared with her mother, led her to her other passions, science and engineering. As a young girl, she dreamed of becoming a scientist, and maybe follow in her father's footsteps by joining the military.

Honey had met Hardcastle while she was doing her engineering degree at the University of O'ahu. He had been lecturing in volcanology while conducting research on the various volcanos throughout the Hawaiian Islands.

Hardcastle had been looking for an engineer to help him create seismic surveillance equipment. An early warning system that could help predict eruptions well in advance, giving emergency services time to act.

The idea had appealed to Honey, as her grandparents had lost their home when the village of Kalapana had been destroyed by Kīlauea, one of the most active volcanos on the Big Island of Hawai'i.

They had started working on a project together, something they had christened *Project: Lodestone*, after the naturally occurring magnetic mineral.

They found their easy-going working relationship soon turned into a deep friendship and mutual admiration for one another's talents.

Honey had encouraged Hardcastle to join her on her surfing and hiking trips. Even though he was 10 years older than her, he was fit enough to keep up with the energetic young woman.

She had also slowly managed to convince him to join her on her more adrenaline fuelled adventures, such as deep-sea scuba diving and parasailing. She had even taken him skydiving a few times, despite his reservations that he was purely a "*land-dwelling mammal*".

Soon enough their friendship blossomed into romance, something Honey's mother was in favour of, but her father was most certainly not.

While Honey's mother had warmly welcomed him into their home, and genuinely seemed happy for them both, Honey's father for some reason seemed to take an instant dislike to Hardcastle.

Hardcastle had noticed her father's influence slowly creeping into their work, with military applications being raised in conversation a number of times.

The military soon became interested in their work.

No doubt due to Honey's father, a decorated General in the US Army, an offer was made that would allow Honey to pursue her dream job of working in the military's research division.

Hardcastle was adamant that he did not want his work being used by the military but was dismayed to find that Honey had already accepted the deal.

Their relationship soon fell apart, much to her father's delight.

"What the hell are you doing here?" was all Hardcastle could blurt out.

"Good to see you too Rad", Honey said in a calm tone.

"It seems I'm in need of an expert volcanologist, so I thought I'd get the best", a smile crept onto her face.

"It's been five years with no contact", said Hardcastle.

"Plus, I don't have any more ideas for you to steal" he said sharply.

The smile dropped from Honey's face at that last jibe. She looked genuinely hurt, then angry.

"I didn't steal anything from you, The Lodestone Project was just as much my idea as it was yours."

"Except I didn't use *our* research to buy myself into a cushy defence job, just so I could please Daddy" he spat.

"My military career has nothing to do with my father's influence." she shouted back.

"He may be a General, but I earned my own way. Never once have I used who he is to my advantage. No shortcuts, you know that." Honey said, a tinge of hurt creeping into her voice.

Far too many times she had had to defend herself and her position, based on who her father was. If anything, living in his shadow had pushed her to work even harder.

"Lodestone could have changed the way we study geology, given us deeper understanding of what goes on deep in the Earth, but you somehow turned it into a weapon", Hardcastle shouted at her, still on the offensive.

Honey's hurt feelings evaporated into annoyance. She was tired of making the same arguments.

"It wasn't just a weapon; it would effectively be a *less-than-lethal* weapon of mass destruction that could change the tide on the battlefield with the minimum loss of life."

"You never could wrap your head around that", she said.

"Yeah right, a giant magnet is going to change the tide..." Hardcastle trailed off at the sound of knocking behind him.

Clayton stood at the front door sheepishly, unsure if he wanted to insert himself into this domestic dispute.

"Uh...Professor, shouldn't we go check out that volcano stuff you were talking about?"

Hardcastle snapped back to his senses, he had bigger concerns on his plate at the moment. Hashing out old grievances would have to wait.

"What do you know about the activity at the volcano?" Honey said, "and who are you?"

"He's helping me with my investigations, he may have witnessed some volcanic activity out in the forest...amongst other things."

Hardcastle didn't know if he really wanted to start trying to explain that whole confusing mess right now.

"Well good," said Honey

"You might be useful to *my* investigations as well."

"What did you say you were here for again?" queried Hardcastle.

"Before you jumped down my throat, I was going to explain that some of our satellites picked up an unexpected blast," Honey said regaining her composure.

"The military likes to keep track of who has nuclear capabilities, who might be trying to develop them, and when any such tests may be occurring. We have a number of satellites that can detect nuclear detonations, especially underground testing."

"I'm aware of it" said Hardcastle, "It's part of the International Monitoring System that was established by the Comprehensive Nuclear Test Ban Treaty."

"I actually gave a talk on the topic not that long ago. I wanted to see if the same system could be expanded to monitor natural events such as earthquakes and volcanic eruptions."

"The way I figured it, if the military can use my technology, I can use theirs."

Honey ignored that last comment, as she continued.

"So wouldn't you know it, one of them detected such a blast a few hours ago. Imagine our surprise when we saw it had occurred on U.S. soil."

"Wait, that loud explosion we heard a few hours ago...was a nuke?" Clayton chimed in.

"The military scrambled to determine if this was an attack from a foreign country or terrorist group", said Honey.

"Upon further investigation, we determined that the blast came from within Mount Arktos, which has confused the situation even further."

"You'll be happy to know, someone obviously was listening to you Radford, as we do keep an eye on earthquakes and volcanoes, if only to rule them out as probable causes."

"However, when a nuclear weapon is detonated, even if it is underground, it sends up a massive electromagnetic pulse that ripples through the ionosphere, something we call *traveling ionospheric disturbance*."

"That's what the satellite picked up on."

Hardcastle pondered what Honey was saying.

That would explain the terrible cell phone service, Hardcastle thought to himself.

"A nuclear detonation from within a volcano?" Hardcastle said incredulously.

"That doesn't make sense, why would someone do that?"

"That's exactly what we want to find out," said Honey.

"Is this just some natural phenomenon, or a matter of national security?"

"Fortunately, I know one of the world's leading volcanologists, who happens to be located right near the site."

"So, they packed me into a helicopter and flew me out immediately to make contact while HQ establishes an operating base to monitor the situation on the ground."

"Keeping tabs on me, were you?" said Hardcastle as he raised an eyebrow.

Honey sidestepped the question, "Rad... I know we have had our differences, but I cannot think of anyone better suited to help me investigate this. This could potentially be a catalyst for war."

Hardcastle thought about it for a moment.

This was bigger than his issues with Honey, and who knew, maybe with her help he could get the answers he had been trying to find the last six months.

The potential destruction caused by an eruption of this magnitude was bad enough without the thought that it was deliberately triggered.

"Okay, let's go" he said, grabbing some gear and placing it into a backpack.

He looked at Clayton, "You think you can lead us back to where you found those bears?"

"Bears?" asked Honey, confused.

"Ah yeah..." said Hardcastle, "There is another matter we might need to investigate while we are there, I'll let Clayton fill you in on the way."

CHAPTER 7

"That's impossible!" exclaimed Honey, as Hardcastle sped down the winding forest track while Clayton let out an annoyed exhale.

"That's exactly what he said!" replied an exasperated Clayton.

"I can't tell you what it was, only what I saw. What I saw was crazy, no matter how many times you make me tell the story, it doesn't make it any less crazy."

Clayton slumped back in his seat as the jeep bumped down the track.

The events of the evening were taking their toll on him. The adrenalin had worn off ages ago, but he was still too on edge to relax. Recounting the events to both Honey and Hardcastle had brought the memories to the forefront of his mind.

It dawned on him that they were heading back to the one place he didn't want to be. He had barely escaped last time, and now he was just going to go back. What if the creatures were still there waiting?

"So...uh Ma'am, you said you were with the army?" he said.

"That's correct" replied Honey

"I'm a captain with the U.S Army, part of the DEVCOM Army Research Laboratory based in Maryland."

"So, you brought guns, right? Lots of soldiers with guns?" said Clayton.

"I make the equipment that helps our soldiers, I don't normally go out into the field, let alone armed", said Honey.

"I flew in with a small detachment to establish a forward operating base. I was dropped off to make contact with Radford."

"Can you call the guys with the guns?" said Clayton as he started to squirm in his seat.

"It'll be ok" said Honey reassuringly.

"We are just going to do a little recon. If there are any issues, I can call in backup."

"Are you sure about that?" said Hardcastle.

"My phone reception has been terrible, especially out in the forest."

"Could be lingering effects of the detonation. An electromagnetic pulse would interfere with cell phone service", said Honey checking her phone.

"Damn, looks like you were right..."

"Do you see that?" asked Hardcastle as he pulled the jeep over and killed the engine.

Stepping out into the inky black night, he stared towards the tree line and let his eyes adjust.

Honey got out and stood beside him, peering into the dark.

"I see it" she said.

Through the trees an orange glow could be seen briefly. The air had a faint smell of wood smoke in it, but tinged with something else, like burning fuel.

Hardcastle grabbed a torch from the vehicle and headed off towards the trees.

"Hey, it's ok if you just stay here. We won't be long" Honey said to Clayton.

The idea of venturing out into the forest didn't exactly thrill Clayton, but neither did sitting alone in the dark. The story he had told multiple times that evening was starting to sound more insane with each retelling. He had to know for sure what was out there.

As they made their way through the dense forest, the smell became stronger. The crackling sound of burning pine needles filled the air.

Hardcastle slid down an embankment and stood in shock at what lay between the trees in front of him.

A helicopter, in pieces all around.

The main fuselage seemed to be intact, albeit now on its side. The tail and rotors were completely gone, most likely destroyed on impact as the helicopter had smashed through the forest canopy.

Hardcastle looked up at the night sky through the dense trees.

Fortunately for the occupants of the helicopter, the densely populated trees appeared to have cushioned the impact somewhat.

Honey and Clayton carefully made their way down the embankment and joined Hardcastle as he surveyed the wreckage.

"It looks military, but hard to fully identify" said Honey as she cautiously approached.

"Hey! Is anyone alive!" shouted Clayton, momentarily forgetting his previous concern as he rushed towards the fuselage.

When he reached the opposite side of the helicopter, a shadowy figure leapt out, slamming Clayton to the ground with a thud. Clayton tried to yell out as a hand clamped around his mouth.

"*Keep. Your. Mouth. Shut*" hissed the figure.

"They might still be out there..." the shadow man said as he slowly released his grasp.

Honey and Hardcastle ran over once they heard the shouting.

Before them, a young Asian man in a ripped and torn suit climbed off Clayton before helping him back to his feet.

"Are you ok?" asked Honey.

"What happened here?"

"My name is Jun Wei," said the man.

"I need your help" he said urgently, as he ducked back inside the wreck of the helicopter.

Hardcastle followed and inside found Jun Wei standing next to another man, his right leg pinned by wreckage.

"Don't worry Professor" said Jun Wei to the pinned man "We will get you out soon."

Hardcastle coughed and covered his mouth, the fuselage was full of smoke.

Clayton climbed into the helicopter and helped both the other men lift the heavy wreckage pinning the man.

Honey grabbed the man under his arms and pulled him free. The trapped man let out a scream and bit down on his fist to stifle his cry.

In the light of the flaming wreckage Honey could see the man's leg was broken.

"I can splint it, but we might have trouble getting him back up to the truck without a stretcher" she said.

Jun Wei ripped up his jacket and gave the strips to Honey to help secure the Professor's leg between two pieces of wood, before slumping down next to him.

"How are you feeling?" asked Honey.

"My head hurts" he replied, "I think I was knocked out cold when we crashed. I have no idea how long we have been here."

Honey took the flashlight from Hardcastle and shone it in Jun Wei's eyes. He winced at the sudden bright light.

"I would say you have a concussion at the very least" she said handing the flashlight back to Hardcastle. "Do you remember what caused the crash?"

Jun Wei stared off into the distance, Honey couldn't tell if he was trying to recall the events leading up to the crash or trying to repress them.

He looked at his rescuers, then over to the Professor lying next to him.

"Can you stand at all?" said Jun Wei as he rose unsteadily to his feet, "We may need to walk out of here."

"I think the best bet is if you stay here, and we send for help" said Hardcastle.

"No!" snapped the Professor.

"We must go now; it is not safe here."

"You are perfectly safe here, now you are free of that wreckage" said Honey reassuringly.

"No!" shouted the Professor again, gritting his teeth as he tried to pull himself to his feet.

"You've seen them, haven't you?" Clayton said softly.

"...the bears?"

The Professor and Jun Wei both stopped and stared at Clayton, mouths open.

Jun Wei's mind raced as he tried to think of what to say.

Then he heard it.

A low metallic growl and the sound of metal screeching cut through the air.

The group spun around towards the crash site.

Then they saw it.

Perched on top of the crashed helicopter, the beast glared at them.

Hardcastle couldn't process what he was seeing, but it looked exactly like Clayton had described.

Flames from the helicopter licked at the creature's body, yet it showed no concern. It's giant head, while in the shape of a bear's, had the wrinkled texture of a cooled magma flow.

Its whole body looked this way. The head and front paws looked distinctly bear-like and menacing, yet its hindquarters were just a giant blob.

The creature lurched off the top of the helicopter and hit the ground with an ungraceful thud, its formless back half engulfing its head and fore legs.

The shapeless blob started to shift and ooze out in several directions towards them.

Two of the protrusions quickly formed back into front legs, as a larger mass reshaped itself into a snarling head.

"We have to go!" shouted Jun Wei as he grabbed the Professor and started pulling him to his feet as he cried out in pain.

Clayton got underneath the Professor's other arm and together they lifted him up.

Hardcastle's mind reeled at what he was seeing.

It was impossible but there it was, right in front of him. It was like some sort of demonic entity from an ancient myth or legend come to life. A creature made of fire and brimstone.

Honey grabbed his arm and pulled him away.

Clayton and Jun Wei had already started running into the dark forest ahead of them, the two young men carrying the Professor between them.

Hardcastle looked back over his shoulder at the nightmarish creature, as it started to charge towards them.

Its semi-formed body slowed it down, but it lumbered with a kind of grace. Hardcastle was aware of how deceptively fast normal bears could move. They were like freight trains made of muscle.

Even so, they couldn't keep running blindly into the forest, especially with the others carrying an injured man.

Hardcastle clicked on his flashlight and scanned ahead to see where the others were. He spotted the trio heading towards a large rock formation at the base of a small cliff.

Hardcastle and Honey shouted at them to wait, that they were heading for a dead end, but they seemed to be moving with purpose.

Hardcastle scrambled over fallen tree trunks, still gripping Honey's hand tightly all the way.

Behind them the creature smashed its way through the trees. He dared not stop and look at how close it was to them.

The trio had slowed down and were trying to catch their breath as Hardcastle and Honey caught up.

"Over there" said the Professor squinting into the darkness.

Hardcastle flashed his torch in the direction the Professor was pointing. The entrance to a small cave was visible.

Better than nothing, though Hardcastle as he ran to the opening.

Lighting the way for the others as they helped the Professor through the small gap, he scanned the forest for signs of the beast.

A tree cracked and fell. Hardcastle shone his flashlight towards the sound. The light reflected off the creature's onyx eyes as it lumbered towards him.

"Come on!" shouted Honey from within the cave.

Hardcastle spun around and started to slide his way through the narrow gap. He could hear the creature right behind him, and he could feel the heat coming from its body, as several hands grabbed his own and pulled him through the narrow gap and into a larger cave.

Hardcastle scrambled backwards, as the Kodiak shoved its massive head through the gap he had just climbed through. The sound of its jaws snapping shut reverberated through the cave.

In the torch light, Hardcastle stared at the creature as it growled back.

It looked like it had been moulded out of molten rock. Its texture looked like so many of the lava fields he studied over the years.

Lava flows had always seemed to be alive to him, the way they moved, the way they destroyed and consumed everything in their path, like a ravenous animal looking to satisfy its hunger.

With a grunt from the bear, the texture on its head started to change. Fissures started to open and glow. Soon the creature's whole head was glowing a brilliant orange. Waves of heat radiated off it, warming the cool damp air of the cave.

"Oh no, I've seen this trick before", said Jun Wei as he pulled Hardcastle to his feet.

The creature's head lost its definition as it morphed back into a blob. Soon the blob started to force its way through the narrow opening.

Hardcastle couldn't believe it, they weren't even safe in the cave from this thing.

The cave appeared to stretch further back. Honey and Clayton were already helping the Professor to move further down the cave.

How far did it go, Hardcastle wondered and prayed there would be another way out? Otherwise, they were all about to be trapped in here.

Hardcastle and Jun Wei caught up with the others as they rounded a corner in the cave complex. He noticed that the ground had become unnaturally flat and even.

His mind raced, trying to look for anything to help them against the impending doom.

Dead end.

The cave ended abruptly in a smooth flat wall, that looked vaguely man-made.

They were trapped. Around the corner the cave lit up with the glow from the approaching Kodiak, waves of hot air proceeding its slow, lumbering movements.

Hardcastle looked at Honey and thought about all the things he wanted to say, all the things he never got a chance to tell her. It was almost poetic that this was how he was going to meet his end.

A sudden whoosh of cold air hit him from behind.

Hardcastle looked over to the Professor who had his hand on what appeared to be some sort of biometric handprint scanner.

A doorway swung open behind him, and the Professor hobbled through it.

Hardcastle looked at the others, and ushered them through it, before stepping through himself as the heavy door slammed shut behind him.

Lights slowly blinked to life, illuminating the sparsely furnished room. It was painted white, and a lone desk sat against the rear wall.

On either side was a doorway leading to identical looking corridors. Next to the doors, some plush couches had been placed. The whole place gave the appearance of a reception area.

The fluorescent lights had all come to life, and a large ventilation fan in the room started to turn, pumping cool refreshing air into the stuffy waiting room.

Honey helped the Professor over to one of the couches and attended to his injuries. Clayton slumped down on the couch opposite them and Jun Wei soon joined him, cradling his head in his hands.

On the other side of the heavy industrial door they entered through, they could hear the muffled growl of the Kodiak as it tried in vain to get through the hidden entrance.

Hardcastle backed away nervously, expecting the door to buckle at any moment.

"It won't get through" groaned the Professor as Honey took a closer look at his shattered lower leg.

"You've got some explaining to do" Hardcastle growled.

"Both of you" he said glaring at Jun Wei and the Professor equally.

"Hey, don't look at me" said Jun Wei defensively, "I have no idea where we are."

All eyes turned towards the Professor who sighed defeatedly.

"This is an old research facility" said the Professor, "we had worked here previously while the new facility was being constructed."

"So, the Dragon's Lair wasn't the only facility in this town?" enquired Jun Wei.

"*Dragon's Lair...?*" said Hardcastle.

"It was the facility located inside the volcano..." Jun Wei started, before realising how much of his father's secrets he was about to share with these strangers.

"The Volcano!" Hardcastle exclaimed, "so you know what caused the seismic activity earlier?"

"There was another lab hidden there, inside the volcano", said Jun Wei.

"It was destroyed by a nuke to try contain things," his conscience starting to catch up with him.

"THAT'S ENOUGH!' The Professor shouted before Jun Wei could say anymore.

"What exactly was this facility, what were you studying and how is it related to that thing that was just trying to kill us?" Hardcastle demanded to know.

"I'm not at liberty to discuss my research" said the Professor defiantly.

"I thought I recognised you," said Honey.

"You are Professor Yong Zhi Shen, are you not?"

"I saw you give a lecture a few years ago at a science symposium. Something to do with *nano-infused biotechnology* if I remember correctly?"

"It all seemed a little too far-fetched back then, but something about your ideas seemed plausible" she continued. "That monstrosity outside one of your little projects?" her tone becoming condescending.

"Those things were a mistake, *a lab accident!*" Jun Wei interjected.

"Oh…I don't know about that" said the Professor, "they are somewhat magnificent are they not?"

Hardcastle turned from the Professor and walked over to where Jun Wei was sitting. Even though he was twice Jun Wei's age, Hardcastle still cut an intimidating figure when he needed to.

"And what's your role in all this?" he asked in a low voice.

"I was just there to observe and report back to my father, I had no idea what was going on in there until tonight" Jun Wei said with a pained expression on his face.

Hardcastle softened his demeanour, this young man had obviously been through a lot in the last few hours, and it was all catching up with him.

"Well, we need to find a way out of here, and for obvious reasons we can't go out the way we came in" said Hardcastle, scanning the room.

"Pretty random place for a front door," said Clayton.

"It is only one of many hidden entrances to this facility," said the Professor.

"Our comings and goings were distributed over a variety of entrances to help disguise the facility's location. But in the end, it was too much of a security risk."

Jun Wei thought back to what he had been told about the Dragon's lair and its high level of security.

"Too many whistle blowers sneaking out hey?" he said as the Professor shot him a dirty look.

"You worked here, so you know the layout, correct?" Hardcastle said to the Professor.

"Of course I do" the old man snapped back, "but I'm not about to lead you all on a guided tour."

"Well, I guess we can always leave the way we came in," said Hardcastle.

"I'm sure you'll be fine on that leg of yours."

The Professor looked down at his injured leg, the pain had somewhat lessened to a dull ache, but he was not going to be able to move without assistance.

"It looks like we are going to have to work together" said the Professor through gritted teeth.

"I need your assistance, and I'm the only person who knows where the other exits are."

Hardcastle stared at the old professor, trying to weigh up his options.

These two seemed to be embroiled in some seriously unethical stuff, but at the same time he needed more information on what had happened inside the volcano.

Sweat dripped down his brow and into his eye. Hardcastle stared up at the exhaust duct pumping air into the room. The air was no longer cool and refreshing.

Still looking up, Hardcastle instinctively backed away towards where Jun Wei and Clayton were seated.

"Uh... Professor, where does that airduct lead?" he said cautiously.

"That particular vent leads directly to the surface..." said the Professor, his words trailing off.

With a groan of metal, the air duct tore open as a large blob of molten rock came crashing from the ceiling and smashed into the centre of the floor.

Everyone jumped to their feet, even the Professor momentarily forgot the searing pain in his leg.

Honey looked past the reforming blob on the floor at Hardcastle. Its massive bulk separating the two groups.

The Kodiak growled and thrashed its paws as it struggled to quickly regain its form, undecided on which group to lunge for.

"Run for it!" shouted Hardcastle.

Honey had thrown the Professor's arm around her neck and together they hobbled down the corridor on their side of the room.

The Kodiak turned its attention towards them and started to pursue.

Hardcastle ran towards the reception desk in the middle of the room, looking for something to catch the creature's attention.

Hardcastle grabbed the flimsy office chair by the reception desk and flung it towards the bear with all his strength.

The chair impacted with the creature's molten head, causing it to deform slightly. The chair burst into flames as the Kodiak swatted it away.

Turning its full attention towards Hardcastle, it charged as Clayton, Jun Wei and Hardcastle sprinted down the other corridor.

CHAPTER 8

Honey could hear the creature roaring behind her as she tried to move quickly while helping the Professor.

He was in a lot of pain, but fear was a good motivator.

She dared not look back, but from the sounds of things the bear was in pursuit of the others. She thought she could hear Hardcastle yelling trying to get its attention and give her and the Professor a chance to escape.

Lights snapped on ahead automatically as they made their way down the corridor.

Smaller offices and labs could be seen through large plexiglass windows on either side of the corridor.

If the rest of the complex was like this, it must be huge she thought, trying to mentally map the facility as they hobbled through the labyrinth of seemingly identical hallways.

The sounds of commotion faded behind them, now all she could hear was the sounds of their footsteps on the metal floor and the Professor's pained grunts and laboured breathing.

"So, what are we dealing with here Professor?" she said, breaking the silence.

The Professor said nothing.

"I could always leave you here and go observe it myself?" she said coldly.

That seemed to rankle the Professor, "You wouldn't dare" he snapped.

"I am, like you, a scientist" she fired back.

"I need to understand what is going on and what we are up against, and you seem to be the cause of this whole situation."

"Right now, the others are dealing with that thing to give us a fighting chance, so start talking!" she spat.

The Professor seemed to ponder this for a moment before conceding.

"The subjects are infused with nanomachines that were designed to repair damage on a cellular level, at an accelerated rate."

"The nanomachines communicate with each other and with the host to maintain homeostasis no matter how severe the damage", he continued.

"They were designed to repair the damage using existing tissues, which is one of the reasons we used bears as a test subject."

"Bears can slow their metabolism down during hibernation. They can go 6 months without the need to eat, drink, urinate or defecate. They are a perfect example of nature's will to survive."

"During hibernation there is no loss of lean body mass because amino acids enter protein synthetic pathways at increased rates."

"The animals show hypothalamic hypothyroidism and increased testosterone production. These changes appear necessary for developing the selective states of anabolism and catabolism found in the hibernating bear."

"In short, all these traits honed over the course of millions of years of evolution have resulted in a creature that was built to survive. All I did was *augment* that natural ability."

His admiration for the mighty animals was apparent,

The particularities of bear anatomy were no doubt fascinating, but Honey needed more actionable information.

"But why are they made of lava?" Honey cut him off before he could start another lecture, she didn't have time for.

"An unforeseen effect of the tissue regeneration process" replied the Professor.

"The subjects were able to create synthetic organs and flesh from inorganic material. We were originally expecting the nanomachines to repurpose existing tissue within the animals to rebuild the damaged and missing organs."

"Not only can the nanomachines perform surgery at a cellular level, but they can effectively act as *3D printers* at an atomic level."

Honey's mind flashed back to the science symposium she saw the Professor speak at. Atomic level construction was the holy grail of nano-technology, allowing people to create anything out of well... *anything.*

The emerging science had the potential to revolutionise technology as they knew it, but it was always seen as being years away from any practical application.

"We were so close to a new frontier in science" lamented the Professor.

"But no... That pretty-faced idiot Jun Wei panicked at the first hiccup and ordered me to dispose of the subjects in the lava flows."

"But it appears that we underestimated the creatures will to survive, it seems they were able to pull raw materials from the environment and the nanomachines then adapted their physiology in ways we couldn't imagine."

Honey stopped suddenly at that last remark.

"You dropped them in a lava flow...while they were alive?"

Honey was starting to see why the animals were so aggressive towards people. She felt aggressive just listening to the Professor.

Honey was surprised by his candour discussing the secretive and most definitely unethical work he had been conducting. She had met many men like him over the years, and the desire to brag about their work was seemingly irresistible.

She felt like leaving the mad scientist to his fate, if it wasn't for the fact they needed his help to escape this sprawling underground labyrinth.

"Wait a second" said Honey, "you said subjects..."

"As in plural?"

"Yes, there are two more out there, although I lost track of them after the helicopter crashed," said the Professor.

A loud roar echoed through the corridor, reverberating as if it was screamed through a megaphone. It was a sound that made Honey's blood turn to ice.

The creature must have lost track of the others, she thought, *and now it had doubled back towards them.*

Whatever the madman had done to it physically, the creature still had its keen hunting instincts intact. It could no doubt smell them against the sterile environment they all found themselves in.

The long open corridors they had been slowly making their way down, would give no protection if the creature caught up and charged them.

Despite having some trouble holding itself together in its bear form, the beast would easily catch up if she was forced to drag the wounded old man along with her.

As much as she would have liked to, she could not desert him. They had no choice but to try and hide and come up with a new plan.

Honey pressed the touch plate on one of the doors coming off from the main corridor they found themselves in. The door slid open, and she helped the Professor hobble over the threshold.

Unlike some of the other offices and labs they had passed, this one did not have a window facing out to the main corridor. Honey hoped that the creature would not be able to see them inside, and she silently prayed she was wrong about its sense of smell.

The room had a variety of monitors and equipment on one side, all blank and lifeless.

On the opposite side of the room stood several large glass cylinders, like giant test tubes.

The cylinders were hinged on one side, and she could see from one of the tubes they opened up like a door.

"Holding cells" said the Professor.

"Reenforced plexiglass, like all the windows in the facility. Shatter proof, heat and cold resistant, you could put even the strongest of animals inside and it couldn't break out" he said with a hint of pride in his voice.

The holding cells didn't seem to be able to hold anything much larger than a person, *most likely used for primate test subjects* she thought with a shudder.

On the far side of the room was a large window looking into a large laboratory. Next to it was a door, but there seemed no way to open it from this side.

Peering through the window into the large laboratory, she could see more of the large glass chambers, but these ones looked like they could hold something significantly larger than the one in their current room.

"Is there a way to open this door" She asked.

"Not without a key card... and I appear to have lost mine in all the excitement" said the Professor mockingly.

Honey groaned at the frustrating design of the facility. It was almost like it was purposely made to be difficult to get in and out of. She hoped the others might make it to the large room and be able to open the door on their side.

There was nothing they could do at this point except wait.

"What were you thinking, conducting experiments like that with no oversight?" she asked, still grappling with what the Professor had told her about his research.

"Bioethics exist for a reason" she said scornfully.

From the small segment of the facility she had seen so far, it looked as if it could support dozens of research teams. Whoever had commissioned the construction had some serious money to throw around.

Enough money they could simply shutter a facility of this scale and build a new one inside of a volcano.

"You couldn't possibly understand what we were trying to create here" said the Professor defensively.

"My research stands to completely re-write the field of biotechnology and medicine."

"Imagine sickness, disease and injuries all being a thing of the past. Instead of evasive surgeries, live saving procedures could be performed at a cellular level."

"People die waiting for organ transplants, when they could have brand new organs constructed inside them, with zero chance of rejection."

"Sure, the technology sounds amazing, but the way you have gone about it means it will never be used the way you hoped it would," said Honey.

That sounds like something Radford would say... Her previous conversation with Hardcastle came rushing back to the forefront of her mind.

"Perhaps you are right," said the Professor.

"My research was funded by those who wish to prolong and extend their own lives. Tyrants terrified by the thought of their own mortality."

"They would see these beautiful creatures as failures, but they have opened my eyes to so many possibilities."

"As a species we could write our own destinies and cast aside the poor hand our genetics gave us."

"This technology could make us...more, it could make us unstoppable."

Honey watched as the old man revelled in his delusions of grandeur, she couldn't tell if he was a genius or a madman.

"You say you designed this technology to help people, but all I've seen is something turned into a weapon..." she said.

The irony of that statement made her feel like someone had slapped her across the face.

She suddenly felt a great need to find Hardcastle, to talk to him, to apologise.

She paced around the room, standing around waiting for either the others or the creature to find them was not a sound strategy.

Honey considered going back out into the main corridor to try and see if there was another way through, but there was no way to tell how close the creature was. It could be waiting just outside for all she knew.

Honey calmed her breathing and strained her ears to see if she could hear the beast. It hadn't exactly been stealthy up to this point.

The room was quiet apart from the faint buzz of fluorescent lighting, but she could also hear a faint drumming noise that was steadily getting louder.

Was it some kind of machinery that had woken up with the rest of the facility, or perhaps the others were close by?

The sound did have a familiarity to it she couldn't quite place.

Honey scanned the room for the source of the noise. It was rattling and reverberating through the pipes leading into the room.

In that moment she comprehended what the sound was, it was metal buckling and expanding due to heat.

As she followed the path of the ducts into the room, the air vent started to glow red hot. The creature had tracked their scent via the vents and squeezed its way through in pursuit.

The air vent burst open violently, and Honey felt a blinding pain as a red-hot claw raked against her arm.

She screamed and staggered backwards, slamming into the locked door behind her.

She instinctively grabbed at her wound to stem the bleeding only to feel fresh waves of pain as she touched the seared flesh. She looked down and saw that the claw marks had been cauterised.

The Kodiak flowed out of the vent and pooled on the floor with a gentle grace.

The creature seemed to be becoming much more adapted to its molten state now. It quickly started to reform its body, its massive bulk filling the room as more of its liquid mass flowed out of the vent, waves of heat radiating off it.

While the bear was distracted with consolidating itself, the Professor inched his way over to one of the open holding cells and slid inside. He grabbed the inner handle of the plexiglass door and slammed it shut.

The cell was cramped, but he felt a sense of relief.

He had helped design the plexiglass, it was specially engineered and could withstand high impact and tremendous temperatures.

He looked over at Honey, back pressed against the locked door leading to the main lab, eyes darting looking for a way out. Even though he was the one inside the cell, she was the one that looked like a trapped animal.

The Kodiak reformed, and stood tall, its head touching the ceiling. It had gotten much better at holding its form together.

Truly a magnificent specimen, the Professor thought to himself.

It was adapting to its new body, learning how to use it to hunt better. *Was this the nanomachines doing, or pure animal intelligence?*

The Kodiak let out a rumbling growl and stared at Honey. Its body was still glowing red hot, causing the air around it to shimmer.

The Professor was fascinated to see what it would do next. Did it need to eat, or would it just kill out of spite or the thrill of the hunt?

Pressed up against the glass to witness what came next, the Professor locked eyes with Honey.

The look in her eyes was defiant and full of anger.

It actually reminded him of the Kodiak when it had been face to face with him in the incinerator room.

The bear stood there for a moment, staring at Honey but sniffing the air. Slowly, it dropped down to all fours and turned towards the Professor.

A hint of recognition seemed to flash across the creatures distorted and burning visage. It charged at the Professor and swiped with a massive flaming claw.

The creature's claws raked harmlessly down the smooth glass of the chamber. It swiped again with the same result. It tried to bite through the glass again and again with zero effect.

The Professor allowed himself a chuckle. It was a fascinating creature, but still not very bright.

In that moment, he regretted destroying the Dragon's lair facility and cursed Jun Wei for forcing him to make a hasty escape.

If only they could have captured this magnificent creature. He would have traded the lives of every researcher and security guard for the chance to study it.

The Kodiak ceased its futile attacks and stared intently at the Professor, and the chamber he had sealed himself inside.

The creature glowed brightly as it started to slump under its own weight back into a blob of molten rock.

The blob approached the glass containment cell and pressed against it.

"Ha, that won't melt it," shouted the Professor triumphantly.

"This plexiglass was designed for space shuttles and can withstand the heat of atmospheric re-entry."

But still the creature pushed more and more of its red-hot glowing body against the glass.

The Professor's grin soon faded as the sweat started to bead on his forehead, and a panic set in as he realised what it was trying to do.

The temperature inside the chamber was starting to increase.

The Professor pulled off his tie and unbuttoned his now sweat soaked shirt. The air was starting to get harder to breath, as he felt his airways being cooked.

He banged his fist against the glass in a futile gesture and instantly regretted it, his flesh searing as it touched the hot glass.

It dawned on him; he was now standing in a giant convection oven.

A full-blown panic now filled him as he felt his skin starting to cook and blister. His nose was filled with the smell of roasted meat and singed hair. He gasped as he felt his lungs burn from the inside out.

He could feel the liquid in his eyeballs starting to boil, as the last thing he saw was the Kodiak bear staring at him with the same look it had given him just before he had sent it to its fiery doom.

Honey watched in horror as the Professor was slowly roasted alive. Part of her wondered how many animals he had tortured to death in the pursuit of his research.

Once the Kodiak was thoroughly satisfied with the Professor's demise, it pulled away from the glass chamber and the smoking corpse within and reformed back into its bear shape with alarming ease.

Its body had cooled as it reformed and became more solid, but the heat coming off it was still intense.

It turned and slowly stalked towards Honey as she pushed her back up against the locked door, trying in vain to avoid her incoming death.

Honey closed her eyes in resignation and waited for the inevitable. She hoped it would be much quicker than the Professor.

Her mind flickered towards thoughts of Hardcastle and their time together.

Never again would she hear him excitedly speak about something simple like a cool rock he found while hiking or watch him squirm uncomfortably whenever her mother would go on about how handsome he was.

She allowed herself a little smile and shed a tear as she felt herself fall.

CHAPTER 9

Hardcastle sprinted down the corridor after Jun Wei and Clayton.

He had certainly done a good job of getting the bear's attention and hoped he had bought Honey and the Professor a few precious extra moments to make their escape.

He had no idea where they were going or what lay ahead.

Fluorescent lights snapped on overhead as they ran, giving an eery feeling as they ran into the darkness ahead. He didn't know what they were running towards, but it couldn't be any worse than what they were running from.

"Why is this place so hard to navigate, it's like a maze", shouted Clayton to no one in particular.

"I think its deliberate", shouted Jun Wei back to him.

"I think it's to disorientate potential intruders", he said as they skidded around the corner into another identical hallway.

The thudding footsteps behind them grew louder.

"I think it's getting faster," shouted Clayton.

Hardcastle sprinted to keep up with the younger men but knew that any moment they would hit a dead end.

The hallway was lined with doors, but those seemed to just lead to isolated labs and offices, places from which there would be no escape if they got cornered.

Out of the corner of his eye he saw something in one of the rooms through the large plexiglass windows some of the rooms had. He skidded to a halt and backtracked, shouting at the others to wait.

Clayton and Jun Wei stopped and turned back towards Hardcastle.

"What are you doing man? We have to keep moving" Clayton shouted.

"There's a way through here" Hardcastle shouted back, "and there looks to be some solid doors between the rooms."

Jun Wei and Clayton looked at each other, then started jogging back towards Hardcastle as they tried to catch their breath now the adrenaline was wearing thin.

As they approached him, the Kodiak came thundering around the corner of the adjacent corridor they had only come from a moment ago.

It looked a lot more solid than it had previously, it's hindquarters actual feet, rather than the mishappened blob it had been dragging around earlier.

Hardcastle ushered them through the door and slammed it shut behind them. It didn't seem like a particularly sturdy door, especially now the creature had figured out how to run at full speed.

Clayton pushed against a metal surgical table in the centre of the room, and it started to slide slowly.

Hardcastle and Jun Wei got on either side of him and together pushed the heavy table against the door, just as the Kodiak slammed into it.

The door crumpled under the weight, but the heavy table jammed against the wall and blocked the entry. A large snout pushed through the gap and snorted a menacing growl.

The three men scrambled through the next door on the opposite side of the room, slamming it shut and barricading it with tables and equipment.

"Let's hope we don't need to come back this way" said Hardcastle to the others, as they stepped out of the room and into another identical long corridor.

"Which way now?" said Clayton breathlessly.

"Well, that says "Main Laboratory", said Jun Wei pointing towards a sign written in Mandarin on a far wall. It was the only signage they had seen the whole time they were down here.

"I still have no idea what this place even is" said Clayton exasperated.

Now the immediate threat was gone, they were able to take stock of their surroundings.

"I've lived here my entire life and hadn't heard even the smallest rumour that there were hidden science bases underground, let alone one in a volcano."

"These labs have been in operation for decades' said Jun Wei.

"Part of my father's shadier business dealings, but even I had no idea things were this entrenched."

"This is insane" said Hardcastle peering into the multitude of small labs and workspaces.

"How could an operation of this magnitude exist, in secret, on American soil yet under the control of another nation?" he said incredulously.

"Well, it wasn't exactly a secret to the right people" replied Jun Wei.

"My father is the head of the Lingzhi Corporation. They have offices all over the world in nearly every continent."

"While on the outside, they look like just another biomedical and pharmaceutical company, their influence runs much deeper."

"We have all kinds of politicians in our pocket, deals with foreign militaries, as well as the criminal underworld."

'The staggering number of connections was never fully entrusted to me. This was my opportunity to prove myself worthy of that trust.'

Hardcastle was surprised by the young man's candour, especially the ramifications this would have if they ever made it out with their lives.

"You seem surprisingly open about all this" said Hardcastle.

"Forgive me if I'm a little suspicious about your intentions here."

Jun Wei shrugged his shoulders and conceded the point. Even he didn't know why he was unburdening on these strangers. Perhaps in the face of death, he wanted his conscience to be clear.

"You have to understand I had no idea things were this bad," said Jun Wei.

"I wasn't exactly naive about the illegal operations of the business, but I thought it was more mundane things like bribery and stock market manipulation."

"I didn't know they were hiding in a basement making actual monsters."

"These facilities had been made with the knowledge of local authorities, members of the military and government. They were all in on it."

"I thought I was here to survey our facilities, report on the Professor's experiments, and give a kickback to the mayor's office."

"The mayor?!" said Clayton

"You mean to tell me that my dad knows about all of this?!"

"You're the mayor's son?" enquired Jun Wei.

"Huh... I guess we both didn't know what kinds of shady dealings our fathers were into."

"Actually, that makes a lot of sense now" said Hardcastle.

"Explains why I always got the run around from your father's office when trying to get permits to study the volcano."

"I guess they didn't want anyone discovering their dirty little secret."

The trio crept down the corridor, listening intently for any signs the Kodiak had found its way through.

Hardcastle continued to peer through windows into the deserted labs and offices as they walked down the corridor, looking for any kind of way out. The whole place was eerily quiet apart from their footsteps and the faint hum of the overhead lighting.

"So why is this place so empty?" he asked.

"My guess is they abandoned it once the new facility was constructed inside the volcano," said Jun Wei.

"Maybe they had it as a backup, just in case they needed it? That would explain why everything was left in standby mode."

"They would need to get the facility up and running again quickly if they were to return here."

"I still can't believe you built a laboratory inside of a volcano" said Hardcastle.

"I would have loved to have working in a place like that...under different circumstances."

"Yeah, well it felt like I was trapped in the bowels of hell," said Jun Wei.

"I'm sure it's great if you are really into volcanoes"

Clayton had to laugh at that last comment.

"Trust me, he's super into volcanoes."

"Except when they are about to erupt, or end up creating deadly volcano...bears," said Hardcastle

"Bearcano's?" Clayton suggested.

Hardcastle laughed at the suggestion and felt his tension ease a little.

"Did you really nuke the volcano?" asked Clayton.

"It was some sort of failsafe," said Jun Wei.

"The facility was lost, and the Professor couldn't risk what was going on there getting out and being made public, so they set off a self-destruct sequence."

"I was told that the blast would be contained within the volcano?"

"It was," said Hardcastle, "except the blast seems to have destabilised the internal structure of the volcano and we are looking at an imminent eruption."

A fresh wave of guilt washed over Jun Wei's face.

"But before we can worry about that, we first need to get the hell out of this place," said Hardcastle.

At the end of the corridor stood a large blast door. The controls next to it lay dormant and covered with a thin layer of dust.

Hardcastle tugged at a small lever on the control panel and the door started to groan to life. The door hissed and slowly started to retract upwards towards the roof.

"Wow, I'm glad we're not in a hurry" remarked Clayton.

"Guess this place hasn't been used in a long time."

After what felt like a minute, the heavy door had fully retracted, and the lights blinked on. Hardcastle cautiously stepped through and surveyed the room.

The room was a large laboratory.

There were dozens of individual workstations and operating tables dotted around the room.

On the far side of the room was another large blast door, already open. Along the wall to their left were large glass cells. Various pipes ran along the wall and fed into the chambers.

Next to the chambers were large tanks filled with liquid. On closer inspection they could see various organs floating inside.

Hearts, lungs, livers, brains, some way too big to be human, all preserved in what Hardcastle guessed was formaldehyde.

"What kind of nightmare factory is this?" Clayton said, trying to take it all in.

Next to the tanks of formaldehyde, there was another plexiglass chamber, smaller than the others, and frosted over from the inside.

The case was filled with all kinds of frozen animal heads. lions, gorillas, wolves, bears. It looked like a grim combination of a meat locker and a trophy cabinet.

"This is some pretty sick shit," said Clayton as he turned away from the case in disgust.

"I had no idea," said Jun Wei transfixed at the sight.

Jun Wei thought back to the operation on the Grizzly he had witnessed, and the callous disregard for the animal that the scientists had as they sliced out organs and marvelled at their own ingenuity.

The bear's subsequent rampage had been horrible to watch, but could he blame it?

How many years had they been cutting up animals for their own twisted agender?

It probably wasn't smart to have told Hardcastle and Clayton so much about his father's business, or its involvement in the current situation, but in that moment if felt good to take a stand against his father for once in his life.

This whole trip had put a lot of things into perspective for him.

A crash and a muffled scream behind them, dragged them away from the grim spectacle of the display cases.

On the far side of the room was a door and next to it a large window. Hardcastle looked at the window and saw the Professor climbing into a smaller version of the plexiglass cells they had in the lab they were currently in.

Hardcastle ran to the window and peered in. Just to the edge of his vision he could see Honey backed up against the door, eyes transfixed in horror.

The Kodiak had apparently lost interest in Hardcastle once he was able to give it the slip and had gone back to hunting the others. It had found them.

Hardcastle grabbed the handle of the door next to the window, but the door held firmly. Next to the door was a small reader that looked like it required a swipe card.

"We need to get this door open now!" he shouted to the others.

"It needs a card to open, look around and see if there is one, Hurry!"

Hardcastle watched in horror as the Kodiak pushed its molten flesh against the Professor's hiding spot and roasted him alive.

Jun Wei and Clayton spread out across the room in a desperate search.

Clayton rummaged through empty filing cabinets dotted around the room.

On the far wall, near where they first entered the room, Jun Wei spotted something dangling from a hook on the wall.

It was a card attached to a lanyard. It looked similar to the ones he had seen the Dragon's Lair personnel wearing.

A small yellow post-it note was stuck to it; the note read *"Left this here for you. Save you the long walk around."* There was a small smiley face drawn under the message

"I found one!" shouted Jun Wei from across the room, as he sprinted towards Hardcastle, the lanyard dangling from his hand.

Hardcastle took the card from him, and with hands trembling, ran it through the card reader.

The card reader flashed a red light in protest.

He peered through the glass window and saw the Kodiak had reformed and was steadily approaching Honey on the other side of the door.

He held up the card and examined it. The magnetic strip was facing the opposite side to how he first thought. He flipped the card over and ran it through the reader.

This time he was rewarded with a loud beep and a green light, as the locks on the door disengaged and it swung open sharply.

Honey tripped backwards through the open door and into his open arms, as Clayton and Jun Wei both slammed into the open door, pushing it closed as the locks re-engaged.

Honey slowly opened her eyes, not sure what to expect.

Instead of her nightmarish killer, she saw Hardcastle smiling down at her, a look of relief on his face. She had never felt so happy to see him.

He slowly helped her to her feet. She turned back towards the window and let out a yell as the Kodiak stood there, its massive head taking up most of the window.

The Kodiak raked its claw harmlessly down the plexiglass window a few times, and then retreated back into the centre of the small room to pace, never once taking its eyes off the group.

"Oh my god, the Professor..." exclaimed Clayton as he saw the charred body.

"That guy was an arsehole" said Jun Wei with a shrug.

He had seen too much carnage in the last 24 hours to feel sorry for the man responsible for all of it.

"Uh...guys" said Clayton panicked, "back up, it's going to charge!"

The group jumped back from the window as the Kodiak smashed its full weight into the window.

Jun Wei let out a little laugh when the bear bounced off harmlessly.

"I've seen what that type of glass can withstand, we'll be fine" he said with a smirk.

"Yeah...but how strong is the wall?" said Hardcastle pointing to a small crack running from the corner of the window up onto the wall, as the bear backed up for another charge.

As the bear slammed into the glass for the second time, the concrete around the edge of the window disintegrated.

The large, thick pane of glass thudded to the floor.

The Kodiak immediately glowed bright orange as its body shifted back to a molten form and it squeezed the bulk of its body through the hole in the wall.

The group scattered.

Hardcastle and Jun Wei made a run for the exit they had seen on the far side of the room when they first entered.

Clayton had turned the other way and ran the opposite direction, while Honey backed up towards the holding cells and the grisly collection of preserved body parts.

They all froze as the bear stood up on its hind legs and surveyed the room.

To Jun Wei it looked even bigger than he remembered it. As if the transformation has increased its size.

The creature turned its head in his direction and sniffed the air.

The Kodiak let out an aggravated roar and swiped its paw through the air. Burning hot droplets of magma sprayed across the room in all directions, igniting everything it came in contact with.

Honey ducked down behind a workstation as the bear launched another flaming salvo in her direction.

The flaming globs of molten rock smashed through the tanks filled with formaldehyde.

The tanks erupted into massive fireballs. Honey rolled under a desk, narrowly avoiding being covered in the flaming liquid.

The fire spread quickly.

As other volatile chemicals ignited, plumes of harsh chemical smoke filled the air.

Sensors within the laboratory detected the smoke and sounded an alarm.

A robotic voice croaked over the aging intercom.

Hazardous material warning, this area will now be sealed.

The toxic fumes were becoming thick and darkening the room.

In a matter of moments all hell had broken loose, it was getting hard to see and to breath, and in the centre of it all, stood the nightmarish flaming Kodiak.

Hardcastle heard a slow mechanical groan and looked up to see the blast doors slowly descending to seal the room.

The doors were closing just as slowly as they opened. Jun Wei and himself were safe, but he had lost sight of Honey and Clayton in the commotion.

Hardcastle spotted Honey crawling towards them, keeping low to avoid breathing in the toxic smoke. He ran to her and helped her towards the exit. Through the thick smoke, he could see Clayton trying to keep low and weave his way through the debris. The Kodiak stood in his way.

There was no way Clayton would make it unless he could distract the Kodiak once again, thought Hardcastle. Once these doors sealed it would mean the end for anyone trapped inside.

Hardcastle estimated he only had a few seconds before the door fully closed. He could certainly make it to the bear and distract it, saving Clayton, but he was unsure if he could make it back to the door in time.

Time slowed as he weighed up his odds of survival, when a hand grabbed him on the arm.

Jun Wei pulled him back towards the door, which was halfway closed now and continuing its slow descent. He had a fire axe in his hands that he had found in a fire evacuation point on the other side of the blast door.

"Let me go get him," said Jun Wei

Hardcastle was about to protest, but the young man stood resolute.

"This whole thing is just as much my fault as well" he said as he pushed Hardcastle back towards the blast door, as Honey scrambled past them.

Jun Wei took a deep breath. His head still pounded, and his body ached. He felt as if he had been running nonstop for days.

His mind flashed to all the carnage he had witnessed in the last 24 hours at the claws and fangs of these monstrosities, monsters he had played a part in releasing on the world.

He thought of the scientists ripped apart in front of him, the soldiers that were trapped when they had locked them out of the control room, the pretty, young admin clerk he was too scared to try and save.

He was tired.

Tired of watching others die while he managed to escape punishment. That might be the type of underling that would serve his father's interests best, but it was not who he wanted to be.

Clayton coughed and spluttered, his eyes stung, but his heart froze as he looked up to find the massive Kodiak standing over him.

The beast lifted one massive paw to deliver a killing blow, when Jun Wei came charging through the smoke and slammed the axe into the creature.

"Go, run!!" he shouted.

Clayton pushed himself to his feet and ran blindly through the smoke in the direction Jun Wei had appeared.

He could see the door only a few feet from closing, so he dived and slid towards the gap.

Honey and Hardcastle pulled him under and to his feet as the door slammed shut behind him.

Staring into the now sealed lab through the porthole on the door, Hardcastle watched as Jun Wei backed away from the bear towards the holding cells, swinging the axe wildly in an attempt to keep the creature at bay.

The Kodiak lashed out and raked its flaming claws across his chest.

Jun Wei cried out in pain as his chest ripped open and seared shut all in an instant. He slumped against the pipes and tubes feeding out of one of the holding cells.

His vision clouded and narrowed. His ears rung and his mouth was filled with the taste of blood.

In that moment, his attention was drawn to a group of gas canisters stacked together, all hooked together and feeding their contents into the pipe he was currently supporting himself on.

The canisters all had the same symbol on them, a little picture of a snowflake, with a large 'N' stamped next it.

A flash of inspiration came to him as the symbol's meaning dawned on him.

As the Kodiak clamped its massive jaws around his head to deliver the killing blow, with his last ounce of strength he slammed the axe down onto the pipe. The spray of compressed liquid nitrogen engulfed them both.

Hardcastle watched them disappear in a white cloud. Moments later, now that the room was sealed, industrial fans sucked all the toxic fumes, smoke and oxygen out of the room, instantly snuffing out the flames.

As the room cleared, they could see the outcome of Jun Wei's sacrifice.

The Kodiak was frozen completely solid, Jun Wei still locked in its jaws.

The creature was eerily still, like a giant statue. Massive cracks covered it as its super-heated body was rapidly cooled from red hot to below zero, all in an instant.

There was no movement, no life in its onyx eyes. It was dead.

CHAPTER 10

"I can't believe he came back to save me," said Clayton dazed as he slumped against a wall. "He barely knew me, he traded his life for mine, just like that."

Hardcastle didn't know what to say. It had been an incredibly brave, yet fatal act.

He was about to run back in himself when Jun Wei had stopped him and took matters into his own hands. An act that had ultimately saved Hardcastle and Clayton, as well as putting a stop to the rampaging monster.

"I think he was trying to undo some of the damage he and that twisted professor had unleashed" said Honey, wincing as Hardcastle attended to the wound on her arm.

They had found a first aid station just up the hallway from the lab, next to the fire safety station Jun Wei had grabbed the axe from. It had been well stocked to treat a variety of industrial accidents.

Hardcastle gently tended the cauterised claw marks on Honey's arm. He rinsed them clean with saline then dressed the wound with a non-stick bandage.

Honey gritted her teeth and flexed her arm and wiggled her fingers. It didn't seem as if she had any nerve or tendon damage. If her reaction time had been half a second slower, she could have lost the whole arm.

It was going to leave one hell of a scar, but she was lucky this was the extent of her injuries considering how close to death she had come.

The image of Professor Yong Zhi's smoking corpse flashed in her mind.

"We need to find a way out of here" said Hardcastle as he packed away the first aid kit, "but the only two people who might have had any idea on how to get out of this labyrinth are now dead."

"Why not take the fire escape to the designated evacuation point?" said Clayton calmly.

Hardcastle stared at him, not sure what to make of the suggestion, when Clayton pointed to something over his shoulder.

Hardcastle turned around to look and saw that on the wall next to the fire safety station was a map, showing an evacuation route in case of emergencies.

The details of the floorplan were intentionally vague. No names for the different areas of the lab, or even the full extent of the lab's layout, but it did indeed show a clear exit point they could navigate to from where they were currently situated.

It might have been an unethical nightmare factory when the facility was up and running, *but at least they took workplace health and safety seriously*, thought Hardcastle.

From what little detail he could make out on the map, if they continued along their current corridor, it would lead into another large room, another lab Hardcastle guessed.

From that lab, there was a set of stairs that led up to a sealed cover leading back outside.

It seemed straightforward enough.

The emergency lockdown of the lab had triggered some warning lights to spring to life. He hoped it was just a matter of following them to freedom.

The trio carefully made their way down the hallway, moving slower than intended as the adrenaline had worn off and the fatigue set in.

Hardcastle wondered what time it was and how long they had been stuck down there.

The facility was deathly quiet now, which made it feel even more unnerving.

At the end of the corridor, another bulkhead door followed by a closed set of double doors led into another large laboratory.

Hardcastle shivered as they walked into the room, the place was freezing.

The room was lined with machinery and large chemical tanks. There was a layer of frost over everything, and he could see their breath as they gasped at the sudden drop in temperature.

"Ah goddamn it's cold!" shouted Clayton, vigorously rubbing his arms.

"First we nearly get roasted to death, now we're going to freeze."

"It's some sort of cryogenics lab", said Honey examining the machinery with interest.

"My guess, this is where they produced all the coolant they were using in the other lab."

"This would have been useful about 15 minutes ago" said Clayton looking at a rack of cylinders, all sporting the same snowflake icon.

"I'm taking one...just in case," he said picking up a smaller, narrower cylinder and slinging it over his shoulder.

"There are more of those things out there remember?" he said.

Hardcastle recalled the unbelievable story Clayton had told them on the drive from his cabin.

He had seen at least three of the creatures. Hardcastle prayed there were only three, and none of the others had managed to make their way down here with them.

Hardcastle snapped back to attention just in time to dodge the cylinder that Clayton was now carelessly carrying on his shoulder.

"Watch where you are going with that thing," Hardcastle said admonishingly.

"Don't get too close to those machines over there with that thing Clayton" said Honey, pointing to two large machines.

"Those are magnetic refrigeration units; they'll rip that cylinder right out of your hands if you get too close."

"Magnetic what?" Clayton said confused, but backed away from them nonetheless, still cradling his prized liquid nitrogen tank.

"Magnetic refrigerators" Honey repeated,

"I have some in my lab back home. We use them in our research on super cooled semiconductors."

"Unlike normal refrigerators, they don't use coolant or gases to create low temperatures, but instead use oscillating magnetic fields to produce an endothermic effect."

Hardcastle was aware of the technology but had never seen such a large one built on an industrial scale before.

They had appeared to have turned on automatically when power was restored to the facility and were the reason the room was so cold.

He marvelled at how cold such a large room had become in such a short amount of time, when he noticed a flashing light on the wall above an unmarked door.

"I think that's our way out" he said, nodding his head in the direction of the light, his hands tucked under his armpits for warmth.

They hastily made their way to the door. The cold was starting to bite into them, none of them were dressed appropriately for the freezing temperatures, it being the middle of summer and all.

Hardcastle suddenly had a realisation. He thought back to his conversation with Clayton's father the mayor, about not wanting to cancel the tourist-busy public holiday due to Hardcastle's concerns about Mount Arktos.

If a potential volcanic eruption wasn't enough danger to the public, what was he going to say about bio-engineered bears made of lava?

He could hardly believe what he had just witnessed himself, despite the various scorch marks and singed hair he now sported.

The more he thought about it, the more he was convinced that the mayor was in on it all, or at the very least, turned a blind eye to what was going on.

There is no way that a complex of this size and sophistication could have been built in secret, let alone another secret base in a volcano of all things.

It all started to make sense to him now. The constant run around he got when applying for permits, he was being deliberately kept in the dark.

If he had not conducted his own experiments in secret, it's doubtful anyone would have raised the alarm as to the potential catastrophe the volcano presented.

Jun Wei had mentioned part of his visit was to meet with the mayor. No doubt to pay him to keep his mouth shut and continue business as usual.

Hardcastle wondered how much Clayton was aware of his father's shady dealings. The poor kid seemed to be just as confused as he was.

If they managed to make it out of here in one piece, there was some serious explaining needed from the mayor's office.

They made their way up a narrow winding staircase, illuminated by dozens of little flashing alarm lights. The air was starting to warm up, indicating they were getting closer to the surface.

The adrenaline had long worn off and his legs were starting to burn with lactic acid. Hardcastle's body felt stiff and sore and all he wanted to do was sleep. It had been a long night.

Finally, they reached the top of the stairwell.

There was a small ladder leading up to a hatch in the roof. Hardcastle climbed up first to inspect it.

There was a long bolt securing the trapdoor from the inside. Hardcastle gave it a tug and it slid out easily. The door swung inwards with a clang.

Fresh air rushed in and Hardcastle felt splashes of water hit his face as he climbed up through the opening.

The air was warm as he emerged from the hole in the ground. The concrete lip of the hatch protruded out from a small creek.

Water flowed lazily around the hidden exit, which he assumed was placed in such a location to help disguise it from inquisitive eyes. *How many more entrances were hidden around the place?* he thought to himself.

Hardcastle splashed the cool creek water on his face as the others climbed out from the fire escape.

They appeared to be under a bridge. Hardcastle hoped that it was close to town, as they needed to sound the alarm.

After they had caught their breath, Hardcastle tiptoed carefully through the ankle-deep water to the far side of the creek, then slowly trudged up the embankment to get a sense of where they were.

The sun was just starting to creep over the horizon as morning broke.

He had lost all sense of time down in the labyrinthian laboratory. He squinted into the faint morning glow and tried to get his bearings. He had only lived in town for the last few months and hadn't yet fully learned the lay of the land.

Clayton climbed the embankment and joined him at the top as Honey trailed behind, hindered by the pain in her arm.

"How far out of town are we?" Hardcastle said.

"We are not that far actually" replied Clayton, surveying the area.

"I'd say maybe 15-20 minutes down the road if we hurry", he grunted as he shifted the liquid nitrogen canister he was still lugging about to his other shoulder.

The lab had spanned further underground than they had first though, but it had worked in their favour.

They needed to report what they had experienced to the authorities, as long as they too weren't in the pocket of the mayor already.

"Still no service" said Honey, checking her cell phone.

They made their way along the road to town. The early morning was calm apart from a few early birds chirping about the worms they must have caught.

It was peaceful, Hardcastle thought, the sounds of nature filling the air. A stark contrast to the deafening quiet of the abandoned laboratory.

Soon the sound of birds gave way to another, a popping sound that was getting louder.

The sound of gunfire.

Hardcastle broke into a jog, adrenaline surged through his body once more at the sound. His fight-or-flight reflex in full swing again.

It felt strange to be running towards the sound of gunfire, but what choice did they have?

The rhythmic *pop-pop-pop* of automatic weapons fire indicated that it was perhaps the police or hopefully the military. Hardcastle was confident they had control of the situation.

The screams made him far less confident.

He was getting closer to town, the shouts and sounds of gunfire all mixing together with loud crashes and dull raspy grunts.

Honey was keeping pace with him now, a determined look on her face twinged with pain. Clayton lagged behind them, reluctant to leave his damned nitrogen cannister.

Hardcastle was stunned at the mayhem that greeted him as he reached the source of the gunfire. Cars were flipped over and on fire, buildings were smashed, broken and bloody corpses littered the street.

Bullets pinged off a nearby wall, as Honey dragged him behind the safety of a flipped vehicle.

Whoever was firing wasn't doing a particularly good job at aiming, either that or they were simply shooting at anything that moved.

Cautiously, Hardcastle peeked around the side of the car to get a better look.

A lone police officer, panic stricken, fumbled with a new clip for his rifle. He slowly backed away as he tried to reload, *but from what?* Hardcastle couldn't see, as more destroyed cars blocked his view.

Keeping low, Hardcastle scurried over to the safety of another destroyed car.

Something had rampaged through this area, destroying everything in its way. His mouth went dry as he saw familiar looking claw marks on the roof of the vehicle.

From his new vantage point, he saw it.

Another one of the bears, smaller than the one they had just faced. This one didn't seem to be molten like the last one, but instead appeared to be made of solid black rock.

The police officer slapped in a new clip and screamed madly as he unloaded on the advancing creature.

Bullets pinged off the creature's rocky exterior, only making the most superficial of impact, as tiny chips of black rock flew off with each hit.

The Black bear let out another raspy grunt as it charged.

Hardcastle was surprised by how fast it moved, considering its appearance. He knew that bears could get up to speeds of 35mph, but this thing seemed to move even faster than that.

The police officer dived to the side as the bear charged, narrowly avoiding being hit.

The Black bear slammed into a police car, crumpling it as if it were made of tinfoil.

The bear was unfazed by the impact and quickly turned towards the fallen police officer. The officer managed to sit up into a seated position, firing again as the bear charged.

The rifle clicked audibly as the magazine ran dry.

The officer barely had time to let out a strangled cry as the Black bear trampled him into the road.

Hardcastle turned away as the man's mangled body was flung aside in the wake of the charging beast.

The Black bear came to a halt and stared around at the devastation.

Hardcastle counted at least a dozen bodies, some little more than lumps of raw meat, while others were more recognisable in their police unforms.

It looked like they had been completely overwhelmed by the creature, their police-issue .22 AR-15 rifles proving ineffective against the bear's tough exterior.

The bear stalked along the street, onyx eyes scanning for its next target.

Hardcastle kept low to the ground, trying to keep out of sight of the creature, lest he draw its attention.

Honey had quietly slipped over to a nearby police cruiser. Carefully she checked the doors and found the driver's side unlocked. Fortunately, the previous driver had left the keys in the ignition.

Silently she caught Hardcastle's eye and beckoned him over as she leant over to unlock the passenger side door for him.

With only the damaged car he was currently hiding behind between him and line of sight of the black bear, he quietly crept towards Honey's vehicle.

Crouched down low, trying to keep as small a profile he possibly could, he held his breath as if the smallest of sounds would give away his position.

Now out of his field of view, he could hear the creature's stony feet scrape against the surface of the road.

Hardcastle could feel his heart in his throat as he crossed open ground.

His back was to the creature, which terrified him, so he kept his eyes firmly locked on Honey who he hoped would give him an indication if it started to come his way.

Stealthily he made his way through the wreckage, avoiding stepping on broken glass or anything else that may betray him.

After what felt like eternity, he made it over to the cruiser and carefully opened the passenger door.

Honey shot him a quick smile, a look of relief that he had made it safely. Her gaze darted to the rear vision mirror as movement behind them caught her eye.

Hardcastle froze stiff as he heard the metallic clunk and heavy breathing behind him.

Instinctively he turned towards the sound, and saw Clayton doubled over trying to catch his breath, his cannister resting at his feet.

"Thanks...for...waiting for me" he panted, sweat dripping down his forehead as he stood back upright.

Both Honey and Hardcastle stared, mouths open at the oblivious Clayton.

Without saying a word, Hardcastle picked up the nitrogen cannister and threw it, as well as Clayton into the backseat of the police cruiser as Honey started the vehicle and gunned the engine.

The car they had previously been hiding behind, smashed aside and rolled onto its side, as the Black bear charged at the sound of the noise.

"Go...Go...*GO!!*" Shouted Hardcastle.

The cruiser lurched forwards, narrowly avoiding the full brunt of the charging bear. The bear clipped the back of the vehicle, causing it to fishtail as it sped off down the road.

Hardcastle held on tight as Honey expertly executed a handbrake turn around the corner. The determined look of concentration on her face indicated to him that she had a fair bit of defensive driving skill under her belt.

They sped down the main street towards the town centre. Fortunately, this early in the morning, there was practically no traffic on the roads, and most of the townsfolk were still fast asleep.

Flashing lights and blaring sirens came towards them, as two more police cruisers came down the opposite side of the street, towards where they had just escaped from.

Backup that had come too late.

Hardcastle hoped they were packing some stronger firepower, as he watched the cruisers race past them.

As he turned, he spied a gun rack on the rear window behind Clayton's head. It looked like a standard police issue Mossberg 590 shotgun.

He wasn't much of a gun enthusiast, but he sure hoped that the passing police officers had them as well, and it packed enough punch that they could stop the rampaging beast.

"That was way too close" Clayton said, breaking the silence.

"No thanks to you..." muttered Hardcastle under his breath. Clayton's damn nitrogen cannister nearly got them killed.

What they needed to do now was put some distance between them and the creature and hope the professionals could put it down.

His heart was still hammering inside his chest. He was unsure how many more close shaves it could take at this rate.

Hardcastle stared at the concentrated look on Honey's face, "Do you think they can stop it?" he asked.

"With these weapons... *I don't know*" she replied.

"Those officers back there were only using small calibre rifles, and it barely made a dent."

"We need a bazooka or something," said Clayton.

"I think it's time I called in some backup," said Honey.

"We're going to have to call in the military, this is all starting to get out of control."

"We need to go see my dad, maybe he can help," said Clayton.

"We have to tell him everything, that hidden lab..."

Hardcastle thought back to what Jun Wei had said, about the mayor's office being complicit, but even so it would be hard for the mayor to turn a blind eye with one of those beasts rampaging through town.

"He would most likely be at his office." said Clayton.

"This early?" Hardcastle enquired.

"With all the lead up to the 4th of July celebrations and preparations for a busy tourist season, he has been working late and even sleeping over at the office," Clayton replied.

It was worth a shot, Hardcastle thought as he directed Honey towards the mayor's office.

The mayor's office stood overlooking Lake Ursa, the early morning sun creeping up slowly and reflecting a golden glow on the still water.

Honey pulled the police cruiser up directly in front of the building, mounting the curb.

"They can give me a ticket" she said with a smirk.

Hardcastle bolted to the front door of the office. The door was locked, and there did not seem to be much movement inside as he peered in through the glass door into the darkened lobby.

Clayton pushed past him and hit the button on the intercom next to the door.

"Dad, dad! Are you in there?" he said.

Silence.

After a brief moment of dead air, the intercom clicked on, and a woman's voice responded. Hardcastle recognised the voice as the mayor's assistant.

"Clayton?" the woman's voice crackled, "What are you doing here this early? Your father is *indisposed* at the moment, we have a bit of a situation here..."

Hardcastle stepped in front of Clayton and pushed the talk button.

"We know about the situation, better than you think. We know about it all, the underground labs... the experiments. We need to talk to the mayor now!"

There was silence once more, then the intercom crackled again.

"The mayor will see you now" she said, as the intercom buzzed, and the front door unlocked.

CHAPTER 11

Hardcastle followed Clayton and Honey as they all walked through the lobby. They walked down the hallway leading to a stairway to the mayor's office on the second floor.

The office seemed suspiciously empty considering Clayton's previous statement about the mayor's office burning the midnight oil the last few days.

The mayor's assistant was waiting at the bottom of the staircase. Her makeup seemed smeared, and her clothes crumpled as if she had slept in them... *or had hastily put them back on*, Hardcastle thought with a smirk.

She led them upstairs to the reception area just outside Mayor Wallace's office.

"Wait here, the mayor will be out in a second," she said.

Hardcastle spied several empty wine bottles in the trash, and two empty wine glasses sat on the assistant's desk.

Hardcastle was about to remark on this but thought better of it, when the mayor's office door swung open.

"Thank you Genevieve," said the mayor, flashing his trademark smile at them all.

"Step into my office, please" he said, ushering them inside.

The mayor looked like he had hastily stepped out of the shower, his hair still damp.

The mayor seemed to notice the inquiring look on his face.

"You'll have to excuse me; I was just freshening up. It has been a long night of planning for the holiday celebrations."

"No doubt" said Hardcastle.

"Dad, you have to listen to us," said Clayton.

"We were attacked by creatures, bears... *made of lava*, there was a lab, we met these Chinese dudes..." he rattled off, barely taking a breath.

"Clayton, I've told you before I don't have time for your *nonsense*," said the mayor, cutting him off.

"It's all true," Hardcastle interjected.

"There are monstrous creatures out there right now, they are tearing through your police force."

The mayor sat at his desk and stared at them for a moment, before flashing them another smile, but with a condescending look in his eyes.

"I don't know what kind of game you are playing here Mr Hardcastle, but my patience is starting to wear thin."

"Genevieve!" he shouted to his assistant through the doorway, "could you please call Hector at the security desk, I think we may need to escort our visitors from the premises."

Her head ducked back around the office door, Hardcastle could hear her speaking to someone on the phone in hushed tones.

"Mr mayor," Honey tried this time, "We need to contact the army immediately, you have no idea what is loose in your town."

"And who might you be?" said the mayor, turning the charm on slightly.

"*Captain* Meli Goodhams" she responded, "U.S. Army Combat Capabilities Development Command."

"I suggest you hear what he has to say, your whole town is in danger, and you seemed ill-equipped to handle the situation."

The involvement of someone from the U.S. military seemed to have a sobering effect on the mayor, his charming smile dropping from his face.

"I have to make a call," she said, turning to Hardcastle.

"Make him see sense," she said as she walked out of the office, shutting the door behind her.

"Let's cut the crap," said Hardcastle.

"Your assistant already told us you are busy dealing with a situation, and I doubt she was referring about keeping your wife in the dark about all the *overtime* you two seem to be doing!"

Mayor Wallace's eyes met his sons, then darted to the floor.

"I want you to get out of my office!" he shouted in a sudden burst of anger and embarrassment.

Instead of backing down, Hardcastle stepped forward, grabbing the mayor by the front of his shirt and pulling him close until they were eye to eye.

Hardcastle had been putting up with crap from the mayor the entire time he had been in this town. After the events he had been through in the last few hours, his final nerve was frayed.

"We know all about what you have been doing, the secret labs, *the twisted experiments*!" he shouted right into the mayor's face.

"You've been turning a blind eye this entire time while people are creating monsters in your own backyard."

"I don't know what you are talking about," the mayor said with very little conviction. All his previous bluster and bravado quickly dissipating under Hardcastle's stern glare.

"We met some of your associates while fighting for our lives tonight. Do the names Jun Wei and Professor Yong Zhi ring any bells?"

The mayor's mouth dropped open and his body sagged a little as he heard the names. Hardcastle pressed him further, not giving him a single inch.

"What are they offering you? *Money? Power?* Do you even know what kind of death and destruction they have unleashed?"

Mayor Wallace struggled to pull himself free of Hardcastle's grip.

He looked to Clayton to come to his aid against this madman, but saw his son had an equally dark look on his face.

"Is this true dad?" Clayton said, "did you know about what they were doing?"

"Look, I had made some deals with some powerful people, they needed some privacy to carry out their work, and they offered to help me with my political aspirations. You know how it is son, it was just business," said the mayor, his voice had become more pleading.

"I nearly died!" screamed Clayton.

"My friends died; I watched a man I barely knew die in order to save me!"

"They...they had made assurances that nothing like this could happen," stammered the mayor.

"I was told they could contain things if there were any problems."

"Yeah, like a nuclear self-destruct system going off inside of dormant super volcano. That's real smart" said Hardcastle.

"Not only do you have killer beasts roaming your town, but if that volcano erupts, and I have no doubts that it will, then you will have no town left at all."

"They used you, don't you see that?" shouted Hardcastle.

"These people set up their monstrous experiments in your town, while you turned a blind eye, and now you are left to deal with the fallout."

"They don't care about you, or this town, or any one of us. You were an asset to them, *an expendable asset...*"

The door to the mayor's office flung open and a large burly looking man came charging in.

Hardcastle instinctively let the mayor go and put his hands up in weak surrender.

The security guard grabbed one of Hardcastle's arms and twisted it sharply behind his back. He let out a yelp of pain, as lightning shot up his arm.

"Hey...HEY!" shouted Clayton as he rushed over to help Hardcastle.

"Ease up man, come on" he pleaded, as Hardcastle struggled with the guard.

The mayor composed himself with a satisfied look on his face as he watched Hardcastle be manhandled. The balance of power in the room now shifting back to him.

"Genevieve, call the police NOW!" he shouted.

The young lady appeared at the door, phone in hand.

"I've been trying, but I can't get through to anyone at the station" she said.

"The...police...are...busy" grunted Hardcastle, still wrestling with the guard.

"Enough of this" shouted the mayor, "get him out of here, I'll deal with him later," he instructed the guard.

Still struggling, the security guard escorted Hardcastle out of the office and down the stairs, with Clayton in tow.

As they descended into the lobby, Honey had just finished her phone call.

"Hey what the hell, man?" she demanded.

"You too *Miss*," said the mayor, the disdain for her rank and position evident in his voice.

He placed a hand on her shoulder as he guided her towards the front door.

"You better believe I will be having words with your commanding office about this," he said in a threatening tone.

The guard shoved Hardcastle roughly against the front doors of the building and into the early morning light.

Honey and Clayton followed them out into the street, still protesting and demanding the guard to ease up.

Nearby, the sound of a police siren cut through the air.

Mayor Wallace and his assistant had followed the guard as he had escorted Hardcastle out of the building.

"Ah, the police," he said in a satisfied tone, "and fast too."

"But Sir, I wasn't able to get through to the police..." said his assistant timidly.

By now the sirens had grown louder, as the police cruiser came sliding around the corner, tires screeching.

The cruiser fishtailed wildly down the street towards them, as the driver regained control. They had taken the corner at full speed and very nearly rolled the vehicle.

A second later, the reason for the driver's haste made its presence known.

The black bear came charging around the corner, moving just as fast as the police vehicle it was chasing. Chunks of asphalt tore up from the ground, as its paws propelled it along the road.

"What on Earth..." said the mayor, trying to wrap his head around the scene.

The guard equally confused and transfixed, released his grip on Hardcastle's arm, who used the momentary distraction to break free.

Flexing the muscles in his hand to check if the guard's rough treatment had done any lasting damage, something caught his attention from the corner of his eye.

A flaming mass shot through the sky like a missile, as the Grizzly propelled itself through the air before crashing down on top of the fleeing police cruiser.

The cruiser crumpled at the impact before igniting into a massive fireball.

Like a bomb going off, debris flew from the vehicle in all directions, the occupants completely unaware of what hit them.

The mayor's assistant let out a blood-curdling scream, the mayor let out an anguished cry, even the burly security guard audibly gasped.

Hardcastle was starting to become desensitised to the mayhem. The horror of the scene taking a back seat to an overwhelming survival instinct.

The pursuing Black bear slowed as it reached the mangled wreck. The red-hot molten mass on top of the destroyed vehicle started to move, its mass shifting and quickly reforming back into a more bear-like shape.

The red glowing quickly faded as the creature's form took on a rocky appearance much like the smaller black bear beside it, its molten core however, still visible from fissures all over its body.

The larger bear snorted and let out a grunt as it turned its attention to where Hardcastle and the others were standing.

"We need to go NOW!" shouted Hardcastle.

Honey ran to where they had left the police cruiser they had arrived in.

"You need to get the mayor inside, get everyone else who might be there, and get them somewhere secure," Hardcastle said to the guard, who stood there, mouth still open in disbelief, before Hardcastle's shove snapped him out of it.

"Clayton!" shouted the mayor as the guard ushered him and his assistant back inside the building.

Clayton took a long hard look at his father, not knowing who he even was anymore, before turning without a word and running toward the police cruiser with Hardcastle and Honey.

"You should be with your father," exclaimed Hardcastle as Clayton leapt into the backseat.

"Given the choice, I'd rather deal with these monsters" he replied sardonically.

There was no time to debate it further as Honey put the cruiser in gear and floored it.

"We have to get those things' attention," said Clayton.

"We need to lead them away, or else they will go after the people in the building."

"My Dad might be an asshole, but he doesn't deserve to end up like all those others."

Honey and Hardcastle exchanged glances indicating silently to each other that they didn't quite agree with that last statement, before Honey pulled on the handbrake sharply and whipped the steering wheel around in a controlled 180-degree spin.

Honey lent on the horn and flashed the headlights as she sped headlong towards the approaching beasts, trying to look as much as a distraction as she could.

The bears accepted the challenge and broke into a sprint towards them.

Hardcastle looked nervously at Honey, who was a picture of calm and concentration, as she played a dangerous game of chicken with the monsters.

Hardcastle held on tight as the distance between them rapidly closed. He lurched to the side, as Honey pulled the handbrake on at the last minute and executed a controlled turn at speed at the intersection.

As the police cruiser's rear end fishtailed around the corner the Grizzly side-stepped, in what was most certainly a hard coded sense of self-preservation it most definitely no longer needed.

The tail end of the vehicle clipped the Black bear in the head, sending it bouncing off as the rear windows of the cruiser shattered with the impact.

The cruiser rocked on its suspension with the impact but maintained its heading and most of its speed. Hardcastle was silently thankful that he wasn't the one doing the driving right now.

They sped away from the town centre and the mayor's office down the main street leading to the main arterial road that looped around the outskirts of the town's massive lake.

Looking in the rear-view mirror, Honey could see the Black bear had recovered from the hit and was charging after them at an increasing speed.

The Grizzly however, slowed its pace as an orange glow start to emanate from under its rocky exterior.

A deafening boom erupted like a bomb going off from the creature as the blast propelled it high up into the air, like a shell launched from a mortar.

Clayton craned his head out of the shattered rear window of the speeding cruiser, tracking the upward trajectory of the Grizzly. As he had suspected, what goes up most certainly comes down.

"INCOMING!" was all he was able to shout as panic gripped at his throat, not able to give any more accurate instructions.

Honey ripped the steering wheel to the side and swerved across to the opposite side of the road just in time, as the red-hot mass of the Grizzly's bulky body slammed into the road where they were just moments before, sending chunks of asphalt flying with the impact.

The Black bear still in hot pursuit, charged past the molten lump as it quickly reformed back into the shape of a bear and joined the chase.

Fortunately, the traffic was light at this time of the morning, but Honey could see a vehicle coming in the opposite direction off in the distance.

Swerving back to the right side of the road, she flashed the cruisers lights repeatedly in an attempt to warn the incoming motorist of the impending danger.

Another boom rang out, and Honey looked in the rear vision mirror to see the Grizzly was nowhere to be seen.

Anticipating the Grizzly's second incoming aerial attack, Honey swerved from lane to lane to make them a harder target.

She had seen the precision it had, as it destroyed the police vehicle in front of the mayor's office, and having no visual contact with the creature, she had to hope and pray it missed again.

Long beeps from a horn grew louder as they approached the incoming vehicle.

An old looking camper van blasted its horn, almost as if it was scolding them for driving so erratically, completely oblivious to the danger.

Honey sounded her own horn in reply, before realising what kind of vehicle they currently occupied, and turned on the police cruiser's lights and sirens.

The camper van slowed to crawl at the sight of the police vehicles lights and wailing sirens.

Honey let out an exasperated shout, trying desperately to will the occupants of the camper van to turn around and run.

Momentarily distracted by the danger to the other motorists, she had let up on the gas. The cruiser losing speed as it hit a slight incline in the road. The pursuing Black bear, catching up, slammed into the back of the cruiser, causing Honey to swerve across lanes into the path of the camper van.

Slamming the brakes on, the cruiser started to go into a skid as she fought for control, trying to correct the vehicle and avoid a collision with the camper.

A fireball erupted as the Grizzly overshot its target and collided with the camper van.

Honey looked on in horror and regret that she could not save the occupants as flames engulfed the vehicle.

She could see the Grizzly already starting to reform and working to free itself from the twisted remains of the flaming wreckage, as Clayton let out a shout and the rear section of the police cruisers roof buckled inwards.

She accelerated but the steering felt sluggish.

She looked in the rear-view mirror to see what was going on, to find to her horror that the Black bear had not only caught up, but had latched on the rear of the cruiser and was trying to climb up onto the roof.

The shifting weight of the Black bear as it dragged itself on top of the cruiser was making the vehicle feel very unstable, as the suspension rocked and rolled.

She thought about trying to weave the vehicle to try and shake off their unwanted passenger, but at this speed they would most likely flip onto their roof, she feared.

Clayton had slid off the back seat of the cruiser and onto the floor, as the roof buckled under the weight of the Black bear riding on top. He heard a screech as the roof peeled open and a rocky claw punched through.

Hardcastle watched in horror as the bear fished around the back seat with its paw, claws slashing the air like obsidian daggers.

Not being able to reach much, the creature withdrew, before a rocky snout pushed through the hole.

Hot air blasted from the creature's nose, as it pulled out and bit down on the edge of the hole it had made.

As it ripped its head back, the roof of the police cruiser peeled open like a tin of tuna.

Seeing the terror in Clayton's face, Hardcastle climbed from the front seat into the back, in a poorly thought-out attempt to protect him.

As he slid into the rear of the cruiser he saw the Mossberg shotgun, it had been dislodged from its rack during one of the creature's attacks.

Grabbing hold of the stock, he pulled it towards him as he curled into a ball and tried to roll over onto his back in the cramped confines of the now crushed rear of the vehicle.

A rocky claw raked down at him, tearing the headrest of the front seat to shreds.

Another violent twist of the creature's head and Hardcastle was staring up at the sky, as the whole rear of the cruiser's roof tore off.

The bear had moved to the front of the cruiser's roof to get more leverage as it tore through the roof.

The roof above Honey's head sagged under the weight as she slid down into her seat and continued to struggle with keeping the vehicle from rolling.

Clayton lay on the floor of the cruiser, Hardcastle lying on the seat just above him, both of them staring directly into the face of the beast, its stone-cold eyes black like death.

Hardcastle didn't have a huge amount of experience with guns but had gone to the range once or twice with Honey in their earlier days.

He only hoped that the weapon was loaded, as he brought it to bear.

The Black bear brought its paw down in a mighty swipe, aimed right at his head, just as Hardcastle pulled the trigger.

In the confines of the cruiser, the shot was deafening.

Hardcastle's ears rung, and he let out an involuntary grunt as the recoil from the shot sent the poorly aimed weapon back into his ribs.

The shotgun blast caught the Black bear directly in its incoming paw, the point-blank shot disintegrating its arm up to the shoulder joint, sending chunks of black rock in all directions.

The bear let out a pained roar as it recoiled from the devastating blast.

Its sudden and wild movement unbalanced the vehicle, still going as fast as Honey could go in order to put as much distance between them and the Grizzly.

Fighting hard for control, the wheel slipped from Honey's grasp, causing the cruiser to swerve sharply, speed and the uneven weight flipping the vehicle.

Everything went into slow motion for Hardcastle.

He felt weightless as he flew through the air, thrown through the gaping hole in the roof.

He twisted in mid-air, the shotgun ripping from his grip.

He saw the police cruiser roll first onto its side, its momentum sending it rapidly away from him, then onto its roof.

The Black bear, still clinging to the vehicle with its three remaining paws, went headfirst into the road, chips of its rocky exterior flying off, before the weight of the police cruiser on top of it pulverised it into a million tiny shards of rock.

Hardcastle smiled in satisfaction as he rag-dolled through the air.

I got you... he thought to himself as everything suddenly went black.

CHAPTER 12

Hardcastle opened his eyes.

Everything was blurry, his vision swirled as he stared up at the clouds. It was quiet and his body felt like it was floating, his skin felt cold and damp, and he felt like he wasn't getting any air.

His thoughts were jumbled, one moment he was in the back of the police cruiser, the raging black bear poised ready to take his head off.

Next thing, *gunshot... screeching tires... flying through the air... watching the cruiser with Clayton and Honey inside flip and roll... the black bear shattering as it slammed into the road at high speed.*

Memories flicked past his eyes like he was watching a slide show, snapshots frozen in time.

His chest felt tight, and a creeping panic started to well up deep inside of him as he watching the scenes repeat over and over in his mind.

His body kicked into survival mode before his brain did, propelling him upwards. He let out an involuntary gasp as his head broke the surface of the water.

As oxygen flowed into his lungs, his thoughts cleared, and his vision sharpened.

He had been thrown clear of the police cruiser as it rolled at high speed due to the destabilising weight of the black bear that had hitched a ride only moments ago.

Fortunately for him, the force of the ejection had flung him clear of the vehicle, over the guard rails on an embankment and into Lake Ursa.

His mind now clear, Hardcastle swam back to the edge of the lake, moving slowly as he assessed the impact with the water had had on his body.

He crawled out of the water on his hands and knees, coughing violently. The impact had knocked the wind out of him, but nothing felt broken at least.

He looked up at the steep embankment he had been thrown over, and carefully climbed back up to the road that they were on just a minute before.

He could see the police cruiser, now on its roof.

It had rolled a fair distance from the point where he had left the vehicle. Glass and debris was strewn everywhere.

He broke into a slight jog, still trying to catch the wind that had been knocked out of him.

He prayed that Honey and Clayton were ok, his eyes scanning for any sign of movement, human or otherwise.

As he drew closer to the overturned vehicle, his feet crunched and slipped slightly on the loose gravel. Hardcastle looked down to see it wasn't gravel exactly, but a fine layer of ground up black rock.

He saw larger chunks of the same rock scattered all around.

As he reached the front of the cruiser, he saw the shattered remains of the Black bear, reduced mostly to rubble.

He cautiously approached, half expecting the remains to launch at him suddenly in a last-ditch attempt to finish him off.

Nothing moved, even when he kicked some of the larger chunks.

"Honey...Clayton!" he shouted as he got down on his hands and knees and investigated the crumpled cab of the police cruiser.

Hardcastle couldn't see into the back very well, but he could not see any sign of Clayton.

Had he been thrown clear as well? Had he managed to crawl clear already as Hardcastle dragged himself from the lake?

Coughing from the front of the vehicle drew his attention.

Rushing around to the driver's side, he saw Honey painfully dragging herself out through the shattered windshield.

He grabbed her under both armpits and dragged her out.

She let out a pained cry, "my...leg" she rasped out.

Hardcastle looked down and saw her foot was twisted at an odd angle, her left wrist also appeared to be dislocated with a blackish bruise starting to form.

Hardcastle supported her as she attempted to stand on her good leg.

It was going to be painful and slow going, but they had to keep moving. They had no idea where the Grizzly had gone, it could already be launching into another dive bomb attack.

Right on cue, the Grizzly slammed down into the ground just short of the back of the upturned vehicle, the force of the impact shoving the cruiser forward several feet, nearly knocking them both down.

Hardcastle eyes darted around their location, looking for cover or an escape route.

The wide lakeshore road left them open and vulnerable.

To their left was forest, they could attempt to try and escape through the woods, but they were in no shape to move quickly through the dense trees.

To their right was the lake, *the cold water might be a deterrent to a creature with all the physical properties of lava*, thought Hardcastle.

There was no way Honey could swim in her condition, but there did appear to be a building a little further up the road, a small boathouse with a jetty.

Hardcastle spotted a small canoe tethered to the side of the jetty. If they could just get to it, they could float to the safety of the open water.

The Grizzly, reformed once again, stalked around the crumpled husk of the former police vehicle. Its attention was not directed towards Honey and Hardcastle, but to the shattered chunks of the Black bear.

The Grizzly sniffed the chunks and pawed almost gently at the remains, letting out a low howl.

It almost seemed to Hardcastle as if it were mourning the loss of its friend. The shared ordeal of their experimentation and transformation no doubt forming a connection between the creatures.

The Grizzly soon turned its attention back towards them as they slowly tried to move towards the boathouse.

The Grizzly let out a terrifying roar as the fissures all over its body glowed red hot. Soon its whole body glowed like a hot coal pulled from a fire.

Hardcastle focused on the lake, half dragging, half carrying Honey as best he could.

"Keep going...don't look" he whispered.

He dared not look back at their impending death. He could tell from the heat on his back it was closing in.

Suddenly there was a loud hissing noise, and the heat on his back was replaced with an icy cold feeling.

Hardcastle wheeled around to see what had happened, only to see Clayton, bloody and battered but very much alive, cradling a metal object... his prized liquid nitrogen cannister.

Clayton turned the valve on the cannister again, and another spray of liquid nitrogen shot out of the nozzle towards the Grizzly. The Grizzly roared and backed away as the cold liquid hit it in the face.

Hardcastle watched the beast writhe in pain and paw at its snout, as the competing extreme temperatures collided.

Clayton ran over to them and ducked under Honey's other arm.

Together they were able to move much faster towards the boathouse and the canoe, Clayton's nitrogen cannister clanging along the ground as he dragged it along with them.

The three of them clanged along the metal walkway of the jetty.

Placing Honey as gently as they could in the canoe, Hardcastle started untying the rope tethering it to the jetty, while Clayton watched their backs, nitrogen cannister at the ready.

The Grizzly appeared to have recovered from its cold shock and seemed pissed. The intention in its body language unmistakable as it stalked towards them cautiously.

Clayton let out another blast from the cannister to keep it at bay, as Hardcastle finally got the knots undone.

The Grizzly having learnt its lesson by now, moved slowly along the jetty to avoid rushing headlong into another icy surprise.

Hardcastle pushed away from the jetty as Clayton climbed onboard.

They floated just outside of the creatures reach as it swiped at them.

The Grizzly, no stranger to hunting in the water, prepared to follow them. As its still glowing hot paw touched the water, it recoiled as the cool water hissed and boiled.

"Ha can't touch us now!" shouted Clayton in elation.

The Grizzly look directly at him, before it backed up a few steps along the jetty.

"Is...is that thing going to try jump on board?" he asked the others.

Hardcastle looked frantically for a paddle, anything that could put a little distance between them.

The Grizzly looked ready to make a flying leap onto them, disregarding the effect the cool water had on its red-hot body.

They were all so transfixed on the creature, none of them heard the whooshing from above, until the helicopter was right on top of them.

The Boeing CH-47 Chinook descended rapidly; its door gunner positioned on the rear loading ramp opened up with his M240 machine gun.

7.62mm rounds slammed into the Grizzly bear, chunks of black rock flying off with each hit.

The Grizzly back away from the hornet's nest of incoming rounds, shifting its body back into a molten state to absorb the impact. The down draft of the helicopter's twin rotor blades pushing the canoe back towards shore.

The firing came to a halt as the helicopter touched down gently onto the surface of the lake, half floating, half hovering, as a soldier tossed a cable with a hook attached to Hardcastle, who quickly secured it to the back of the canoe.

The soldier hit a button on the winch control and Hardcastle had to hold on tight to avoid falling out of the boat, as it sped quickly across lake, up the loading ramp and into the cargo hold of the helicopter.

Once onboard, the loadmaster tapped the door gunner on the shoulder, who proceeded to resume fire on the retreating grizzly, now the package was secured.

The loadmaster spoke into his headset, Hardcastle unable to hear over the din caused by both the helicopters rotors, and the machine gun fire.

He felt his stomach drop as the helicopter swiftly rose into the air, the door gunner moving from his position as the rear ramp closed.

With the ramp closed, the deafening sound subsided somewhat. The loadmaster pointed at his headset and then to the rack just above where they were seated, to where the extra pairs of headsets were stored.

Hardcastle put on a pair, handing another to Clayton, and helped Honey put on a set as a young medic attended to her injuries.

"What's the situation Ma'am?" said the Loadmaster.

"Two of the creatures have been neutralised for certain," she said through gritted teeth.

"What is the status on the third one, did you get it?"

"Negative Ma'am," said the Gunner.

"That is the craziest shit I've ever seen; damn thing just absorbed the rounds like they were nothin'."

"We've been monitoring the situation with Mount Arktos as you requested," said the Loadmaster.

"Is this the guy?" he said pointing at Hardcastle.

Honey nodded with a pained expression, as the medic splinted her broken leg.

"Professor Hardcastle, we've been on standby monitoring the activity at Mount Arktos, and..." the Loadmaster trailed off as he looked out of the helicopter's small windows, towards the mountain that loomed over the town.

"It's getting worse."

The helicopter flew a short distance to the outskirts of town. Hardcastle could see as they descended, a small military camp had been set up. People in uniform buzzed around in a hive of activity.

The rear ramp of the helicopter lowered as they touched down. Hardcastle moved down the ramp and stepped aside as two more medics rushed up the ramp with a stretcher in hand.

The Forward Operating Base was situated on the far side of the lake, the open area giving a clear view towards the now menacing looking volcano.

Hardcastle could see clouds of volcanic gases starting to billow out of the mountain.

Towards him strode a bullish looking man in military fatigues. He had a thick neck, stocky body, and leathery looking face, punctuated by a neatly trimmed grey moustache.

Military personnel stopped what they were doing, came to attention, and quickly snapped off a salute as he passed them, barely waving an acknowledgement in return.

He moved with purpose, so Hardcastle thought, obviously the man in charge around here.

"Professor Hardcastle" said the man as he approached and extended his hand.

"Colonel Deckard," he said as Hardcastle shook his hand, "I'm Captain Goodhams' commanding officer."

"I've been told you are the foremost expert on Mount Arktos, and what we might be dealing with here?" he continued.

"It's strange, there hasn't been a lot of academic research done on this particular volcano, even though I've had it explained to me that an eruption could be as disastrous, if not more so, than Yellowstone."

"I think I have an explanation for why researchers have had such a hard time getting permission to study the area," said Hardcastle.

"Captain Goodhams has advised us of that situation as well," replied the Colonel.

"If it ain't the damndest thing I've heard of in all my years. I'd say y'all were crazy if it wasn't for the multiple eyewitness reports that are starting to filter through."

Hardcastle watched as Honey was carried past them on a stretcher. Sensing his concern, she flashed him a small thumbs up.

Clayton had insisted he was fine to walk, but his legs buckled as he tried to walk down the loading ramp. The Gunner and Loadmaster were quick to catch him and stop him falling down the ramp.

The young medic who had accompanied them on the flight, shone a small pen light into his eyes, then quickly said something into her radio before pointing in the same direction that Honey had been carried off.

Hardcastle had to trust that they would be alright, they had all come too far at this point.

"What's the situation with the volcano?" asked Hardcastle as he walked with the Colonel to a large field tent in the middle of the base.

"We have been monitoring it via satellite, and have been getting strange thermal and seismic readings from it over the last few hours," said the Colonel.

"We originally flagged it from orbit as being a nuclear detonation, but Captain Goodhams identified the site as being a dormant volcano and suggested we try locate you to assist."

"We flew out from Maryland and established this FOB to monitor the situation, while the captain made contact with you and brought you in. I believe you two know each other?"

"Yes... we're *friends*" said Hardcastle, a wave of mixed emotions flooded over him as he thought about Honey. He hoped she was ok.

"You were right about it being a nuclear detonation Colonel" he said, focusing back on the task at hand.

"We met some interesting people who were part of a research facility, located inside the volcano."

"Say again?" said the Colonel.

"The lab was doing some sort of regenerative biotech experiment using nanotechnology. The bears were test subjects that were discarded, intending to be destroyed by lava flows powering the facility," said Hardcastle.

"The bears were transformed into these creatures we have been dealing with all night. They somehow got back into the facility and went on a rampage."

"They couldn't contain them, so they tried to destroy all the evidence and make it look like the explosion was naturally occurring."

"You said you met people involved in these experiments?" said the Colonel.

"Yes" replied Hardcastle, "the head scientist of the facility, as well as a corporate executive…"

"There are a lot of powerful people involved here."

"Where are these two individuals now?" asked the Colonel.

"Dead" said Hardcastle.

The Colonel pondered this as he ran his fingers across his moustache.

"Well, we will be getting you to give us a full debrief on what you have learned, but right now we need as assessment on what we need to do about this volcano," he said.

"I have an evacuation plan for the town in place, say the word and we can start getting these people to safety."

"I think that's wise" said Hardcastle as he looked at the billowing clouds emanating from the mountain.

"We haven't got much time left."

CHAPTER 13

Hardcastle was pouring over all the data the military had been able to collect over the past 24 hours, so engrossed in the task he didn't notice Honey limp into the tent on crutches.

"Any good news?" she said, breaking his extreme concentration.

The look on his face did not look good.

His hard expression softened as he saw her, replaced by a look of concern.

"How are you feeling?" he said.

"Pretty banged up, but I'll survive" replied Honey.

"I've been clawed, burned, banged around and nearly blown up by a kamikaze bear made of lava..."

"Typical Thursday" said Hardcastle with a grin.

Honey laughed and joined him looking at all the data being displayed on multiple monitors.

"That does not look good" she said.

"As you know, typically volcanoes build up to an eruption over time" said Hardcastle.

"But this is different, a nuclear bomb went off and weakened the crust that has been keeping this whole thing contained."

"More and more magma is escaping from below."

"But wouldn't that help release some of the pressure?" asked Honey.

"To some degree" said Hardcastle, "but that magma is further weakening the plug holding everything at bay."

"My research had indicated that the volcano didn't have enough pressure to blow its plug. There was little risk of an eruption for generations."

"But this blast has done enough damage that it could blow now?" said Honey.

"Is there any way to reinforce the plug, make it strong again?"

"I've been thinking about that" said Hardcastle.

"There are new lava vents opening all up inside, filling the central chamber with more magma."

"If we could somehow cool them down, they would form a new layer of rock over the damaged parts."

"But it would have to happen rapidly and uniformly" said Hardcastle.

"Something like water wouldn't work, so trying to flood it is not viable, the water would just boil off before it did any good."

'It needs to be something that can get temperatures below freezing. We saw what liquid nitrogen did to those creatures, but there isn't enough of that available for what we need to do."

Honey's mind flashed to underground laboratory... *seeing the horrific Kodiak that nearly burnt her alive get flash frozen... their escape through the freezing refrigerated labs.*

An idea started to form, "Radford, how magnetic is volcanic rock?"

"There are all kinds of ferromagnetic minerals located in volcanic rock, if you remember my studies on the iron content of the lava tubes back in Hawai'i..." said Hardcastle.

"Project Lodestone," said Honey.

"Lodestone?" said Hardcastle, remembering the research project that ultimately ruined their friendship and ended their relationship.

Honey had that look on her face, one Hardcastle had seen many times before.

She had a plan.

He had learnt early on in their partnership to trust her ideas, or at the very least get out of the way and let her work.

"Come on!" Honey said as she hobbled out of the tent.

Hardcastle stared at the ever-increasing cloud of gas seeping out of the top of the mountain, a lighter colour and different formation, making it stand out against the other clouds in the mid-afternoon sky.

If would have been a lovely summer day, had it not been for that spectre of impending death and destruction floating in the sky.

Honey had called for a briefing with the Colonel and all the top personnel to propose her plan.

A young private interrupted Hardcastle's grim train of though.

"They are ready now, Sir" said the private.

Hardcastle followed the private to one of the base's demountable structures. He felt the air conditioning as he walked into the main room.

A faint shiver ran down his spine at the drop in temperature, but it felt good to be out of the summer heat.

He had felt that he had come close to being cooked alive far too many times in the last 24 hours.

Seating had been set up in the meeting room for the base's key personnel. Hardcastle scanned the room and saw a visible tension in the faces of all in attendance.

They knew, at least to a small degree, the danger the mountain posed, so when they saw him enter the room, all eyes fixed on him as the leading expert to dispel their fears and concerns.

Honey was busying herself with a laptop connected to a projector, as she loaded up a hastily made presentation for the group.

Their idea seemed insane but considering everything he had been through in the past 24 hours; it was probably the sanest thing of them all.

Colonel Deckard strode into the room, everyone apart from Hardcastle snapped to attention, while he just stood there awkwardly waiting for everyone to relax.

The Colonel waved a dismissive hand at the group and people relaxed and took their seats.

Hardcastle stood next to Honey, unsure of how all these senior military staff and scientists would react to their plan.

Honey sensed his unease and launched into their presentation.

"Thank you all" she started.

"As you are aware, Mount Arktos is on the verge of an eruption."

"Nearly 48 hours ago our satellites detected the detonation of a low-yield nuclear weapon. Upon further inspection, the site of the explosion was shown to be the interior of Mount Arktos, causing confusion as to if this was a naturally occurring event or not."

"Intelligence we have procured has confirmed that this was indeed a nuclear weapon, and that it was deliberately detonated in an ill-conceived attempt to cover up a clandestine research facility located within the mountain itself."

The gathered group exchanged confused looks at the revelation.

"The idea was that the blast would be contained within the volcano, and that it would be explained as naturally occurring volcanic activity" Honey continued.

"Unfortunately, the blast has damaged the interior of the volcano, setting off a chain reaction which will only destabilise it further."

"This means that we are working with an unknown timeline for a catastrophic event to occur. We could be days, or even hours away from an eruption that has the potential to be more destructive than anything witnessed in the last 10,000 years."

Nervous murmuring started to fill the room.

"Professor Hardcastle and I have a potential solution to this."

"Professor?" Honey said handing over to Hardcastle.

Hardcastle stepped forward and waited a moment for the murmuring to die down.

"Most volcanic eruptions of this magnitude take thousands of years to occur," he said.

"In this volcano, there is a large plug of solid rock blocking the central chamber. There are smaller vents that allow small amounts of lava to reach the surface, this actually helps the volcano stabilise, as it allows some of the pressure to escape naturally."

"As Captain Goodhams previously stated, we discovered that a covert facility was built inside the volcano, both to use it as cover and to make use of geothermal power to further stay off the grid."

"They detonated a failsafe device to eradicate an experiment that had gone wrong and compromised the facility..."

A hand at the back of the room shot up.

"Sir are those the creatures we have heard about, you know... bears made of lava?" said a soldier.

The room erupted in chatter, some scoffed at the idea, others sounded freaked out by it.

Hardcastle heard the phrase *Bearcano* being thrown around.

Clayton had obviously been talking to people.

"It's true" said the Gunner that had been aboard the helicopter.

"Shot at one myself. Emptied nearly a full box into it, and it barely made a scratch."

Hardcastle held up his hands for silence.

"I don't know what you've been briefed on, but what you may have heard is true. There is still a remaining creature out there, and it is like nothing you could imagine. But the reality is if we don't find a way to prevent this eruption, a bear made of lava is going to be the least of your concerns."

Hardcastle felt himself slip back into academic mode, like he was back teaching first year geology students.

"If Mount Arktos blows, it will release a massive pyroclastic flow, a cloud of gas, ash, and rock moving at speeds of over 400 miles per hour, at temperatures over 1500 degrees. Anything it hits will be flash fried in a second."

"Your skin will be sandblasted from your body, your lungs scorched by toxic gases, your blood will boil and the pressure from all the liquid in your body turning to steam will be enough to cause your head to explode."

"Archaeologists of the future will marvel at our ash-preserved remains, like we do now to the victims of Vesuvius in Pompeii."

The room was suddenly incredibly quiet, and profoundly serious.

Honey clicked onto the next slide of her presentation.

"Some of you may be familiar with Project: Lodestone" she said.

"For those who aren't, Loadstone was envisioned to be a *less-than-lethal* weapon of mass destruction."

Honey clicked onto the next slide, showing a schematic of the device.

"Dropped like a conventional bomb over a target, Lodestone would emit an electromagnetic pulse that would induce magnetism in any ferromagnetic material."

"Iron, cobalt, steel, even aluminium under certain situations could become magnetic. Guns would jam, engines would seize, electronic and navigational equipment would be rendered useless, forcing an enemy to surrender before a single shot was fired."

Honey looked at Hardcastle as she continued, "We are going to use Lodestone to create the world's largest magnetic refrigerator."

Honey elaborated, as she saw a number of confused hands shoot up.

"Using the magnetocaloric effect, we can create a cooling effect to a high degree, many hundreds of degrees below zero."

"We currently use similar technology back in my lab for cooling of super conductor material and can generate temperatures colder than conventional coolants such as liquid nitrogen."

Hardcastle thought back to the underground lab and how cold the cryonics laboratory had been.

"By applying a magnetic field to certain metals, the electrons which are normally free to spin, line up. This constraint of the electrons causes the atoms to vibrate, creating heat. When the magnetic field is removed, the electrons are free to spin and the heat energy is released causing the material to rapidly cool," Honey continued.

"We know that Mount Arktos has a particularly high level of ferromagnetic materials such as iron and nickel," said Hardcastle, "the perfect material to achieve this type of effect."

The group was quiet for a moment, until one of the military scientists raised a hand.

"You said that Lodestone could induce magnetism, but how will you turn off the magnetic field once it is established?"

Hardcastle looked at Honey, then back to the scientist.

"Well, this is where it gets a little tricky," he said.

"By magnetising the interior of the volcano itself, we will see a rapid increase in the temperature inside. The heat will be so intense, the magnetised metals will hit the *Curie point*, which is the temperature in which they lose their magnetic properties, in turn collapsing the magnetic field."

"The problem is, the Curie point of iron is around 1,418 degrees Fahrenheit, which is hotter than what is required to start turning solid rock into magma."

"By inducing the right temperature to collapse the magnetic field and achieve a magnetocaloric effect, we risk melting the plug holding the volcano at bay."

The room was silent.

"So, what you are saying is, we could freeze the inside of the volcano with a big magnet and plug up the hole left by a nuke?" said Colonel Deckard.

"Basically" said Hardcastle, shrugging his shoulders.

"And if we mess it up, the thing goes boom on us?" continued the Colonel.

"It'll go boom on us regardless" said Hardcastle, "It's just a matter of when."

"Captain Goodhams" said the Colonel, "does this magnet bomb of yours actually work?"

"For its intended purpose... not yet sir, but for this, it will be able to create the large-scale magnetic field we need. I'm sure of that," said Honey.

"And where is this bomb of yours?" said the Colonel.

"Back at DEVCOM, in Maryland, Sir" she responded.

"We could have it loaded, flown here and ready for deployment in a matter of hours."

"Well Captain," said the Colonel, "I guess you've got a Volcano to stop."

CHAPTER 14

It was late into the afternoon when the Chinook returned from Aberdeen Proving Ground in Maryland, the home of the U.S. Army's DEVCOM, where Honey had spent the last few years trying to perfect her *Less-than-lethal WMD*.

Hardcastle sat on a stool in the medical tent. After the briefing, he could do nothing but wait, so he and Honey decided to check in on Clayton.

Hardcastle was impressed by how the young man had handled himself through everything and had grown on him over the course their shared ordeal.

He thought back on how they had met less than two days prior, and how easily it could have been for him to have dismissed the young man's outlandish claims of bears made of lava.

It was his forward thinking and bravery that had saved both Honey and Hardcastle as they painfully limped from the wreckage of the police cruiser.

Clayton had hidden his own injuries from the crash well, only finally collapsing from the effort once they had first reached the base.

He had several broken ribs and a fractured collarbone, but seemed to be in good spirits now the painkillers had kicked in.

Military personnel had come to debrief them all and document as much as the trio could tell them about the bears, the underground lab, and of Jun Wei and Yong Zhi.

Word had gotten around base of their exploits, and several of the soldiers came to ask questions and hear Clayton's ever expanding, grandiose tale of terror and survival.

"You know, I think I want to join the army" he said.

"I'll be 21 in a few months, and I just keep thinking how I might never have made it if it wasn't for these army guys, saving our asses at the last moment."

"The military's worked out well for me" said Honey, "I might even be able to put in a good word for you," she said giving his hand a squeeze.

"I'm gonna join the Rangers" he said, watching a group of soldiers getting ready to patrol for any sign of the yet to be accounted for Grizzly.

"Yeah...from park ranger to army ranger" he said with a sleepy smile, his latest dose of pain medication starting to take hold.

Hardcastle stood and got ready to leave Clayton to his well-earned rest.

He helped Honey to her feet, as she grimaced through the pain of her own injuries, having forgone any pain medication herself.

A thundering sound travelled overhead as the flaps of the hospital tent blew open.

"The Helicopter is here" said Hardcastle.

"We'll go inspect the Lodestone in a minute" said Honey, "I need to say a few things to you first."

"I'm sorry" she said, "the Lodestone was your idea, I did take it and use it for my own benefit. I'm sorry" she said, blinking back tears.

"Hey now" said Hardcastle, "If it wasn't for you, we wouldn't have what is the best and only hope we have for averting what could potentially be an extinction level event."

"I would have just used it for something dumb like mapping lava chambers or something."

"Well, when you put it that way..." Honey said, breaking into a smile.

"Seems pretty fitting actually" she said, "using our little project to literally bomb a volcano."

"Looks like we both win," said Hardcastle with a laugh.

They stared into each other's eyes for what seemed like forever.

Hardcastle touched his hand to her cheek, and she gently placed her hand on his.

"There is something else I need to talk you about" she said.

Just then, a young private ran up to them and snapped off a quick salute as she came to halt in front of Honey.

"Ma'am...Sir, they need you at the landing pad."

"Later then?" said Hardcastle as they turned and followed the private towards the helicopter.

The Loadmaster and Gunner greeted them as they helped Honey up the loading ramp of the cargo helicopter.

Strapped down in the middle of the cargo bay was a large device, about the size of a small car. The riveted steel plates along the cylindrical body of the device, reminded Hardcastle of old atomic weapons from the 1950's.

"'Scuse the mess" said the Loadmaster as he stepped over the canoe that they had used to escape the Grizzly on the lake.

"The hook is jammed in too tight" he said pointing to the grappling hook connected to the winch that was used to pull them aboard.

"Need to cut it loose with a blowtorch, just haven't had the time y'know?"

"It's fine," said Hardcastle inspecting the Lodestone device.

"Doesn't look too dissimilar to how I remember it" he said.

"Why mess with perfection?" said Honey with a smile.

"Thing's got a lot of weight to it" said the Pilot stepping from the cockpit.

"It's got a lot of shielding," said Honey.

"Not much good if it starts messing with the aircraft that's carrying it before it reaches its target."

"Just worried about it shifting in transport," said the Pilot.

"What's the plan for deployment?"

"It'll be airdropped directly above the volcano" said Honey, "drag chutes will slow its decent."

"Now, this thing is still a prototype and isn't designed for aerial deployment at this stage. It doesn't have a barometric fuze of any kind, so a timer is going to have to be set manually."

"The target will need to be eyeballed once you are in position and the timer calculated from there."

"You need to make sure you drop it from an altitude that will give you enough time to get clear," said Honey.

"It needs to detonate inside the volcano for this to work. Too high and the pulse won't be contained and is liable to fry all your electronics."

"No pressure," said the Loadmaster.

"Ok, we'll go over the operation of the device with you, so you know how to prime it..."

Hardcastle's voice was cut off abruptly by a deafening boom.

They rushed to the ramp of the helicopter and stared out across the lake towards the mountain, which was now billowing a massive plume of smoke into the air.

A sudden change of plans was now required.

"We need to get going now!" shouted Hardcastle, "That was a warning shot, we don't have much time left."

The Pilot jumped into the cockpit and started up the engines. There was no time to wait for his co-pilot to return, they were going to have to fly with a skeleton crew.

"Ah screw it" said the Gunner as he ran back up the ramp into the helicopter.

"We aren't going to be able to operate this thing by ourselves," said the Loadmaster.

"One of you needs to come with us."

"I'll go," said Honey.

The image of Jun Wei charging back into the burning laboratory flashed in Hardcastle's mind. He wasn't about to let anybody else sacrifice themselves.

"No, you are too injured, you can barely stand as it is," he said.

"We gotta go!" shouted the Loadmaster over the roar of the helicopter's powerful rotors.

Hardcastle ran up the ramp after him, but before he could turn around to tell Honey how he felt, considering this might be the last time they saw each other, they were airborne.

The wind ripped through the open ramp, and the Helicopter soared through the air with haste.

Hardcastle grabbed onto the netting lining the sides of the cargo bay, as the Loadmaster hit the button to close the ramp behind them.

It was quieter now with the ramp closed, but Hardcastle's ears pounded with the sound of his own heart.

The billowing cloud of volcanic smoke and ash towered into the sky, as he stared through one of the aircraft's small side windows.

The Loadmaster tapped him on the shoulder and handed him a pair of headphones. The roar of the engines suddenly went quiet as he slipped them on.

"Ok Professor, what's the plan?" said the Pilot over the intercom.

"We need to get over the top of the mountain but avoid flying into that cloud" Hardcastle replied.

"The fumes are toxic, and the ash and debris will choke out the engines."

"Roger that," replied the Pilot, "this baby can reach around 18,000 feet."

That should keep them above the cloud, Hardcastle thought to himself.

He did some quick calculations of the bombs terminal velocity and determined at that height; the bomb would be in free fall for at least 90 seconds.

Unlike the bomb itself, the parachutes could be set to deploy at a certain altitude. Another 30 seconds descent under the parachutes should put it exactly where it needed to be for maximum effect.

"Right, that gives us 2 minutes" said Hardcastle as he started to input the time into the device.

He would wait until they were in position before he started up the device. He was still unsure about just how well shielded it was, and if it would interfere with the pilot's navigational equipment.

They only had one chance at this.

Another boom belched from the mountain, so loud it could be heard even through the noise cancelling headphones Hardcastle wore.

The helicopter swerved violently to the side, Hardcastle barely grabbing onto the wall netting in time to avoid being thrown across the cargo bay.

"Strap in fellas" said the Pilot, "we have incoming."

Hardcastle pulled down one of the helicopter's fold-down seats, and strapped himself in.

Staring out the window while the helicopter made another sharp turn that made his stomach drop, he could see that the mountain had just ejected a mass of debris in their direction, like a giant shotgun blast.

Chunks of rock flew through the air; the plug was weakening, and pockets of trapped gas were now bursting through.

He could see the flicker of molten magma spitting from the top of the mountain, as rivers of glowing orange lava started to snake from fissures opening up along the mountain top.

The Chinook skimmed low across the lake and veered towards the forest. It was too dangerous to approach the mountain from this direction.

The helicopter gained altitude as it reached the trees, just barely hovering above them, keeping low in case a rogue projectile forced them out of the air.

"Gonna try going wide, approach from another direction" said the Pilot over the intercom.

A fountain of lava spat from a fissure on the face of the mountain they had been approaching from. That had been the most direct route, but safety was just as important as speed in this matter.

The helicopter rocked violently and started to spin.

Hardcastle felt his ribs crush against the harness with the centrifugal force of the spinning aircraft.

The pilot quickly corrected the spin, narrowly avoiding hitting the treetops.

"Whoa, we took a hit there, boys" he said with strain in his voice.

"Something big just smashed into us, but we're ok."

"I'm taking her up, too dangerous down here."

The helicopter lifted up, a little slower than before thought Hardcastle, but maybe everything was just moving in slow motion at this point with all the adrenaline surging through him.

They gained altitude steadily, slowly circling back around, over the lake and toward the mountain.

"Ah, Professor..." said the Pilot over the intercom, "you might want to see this."

Hardcastle undid his harness and carefully made his way towards the cockpit. He slid into the empty co-pilot's chair and stared out the window.

The plume of volcanic ash was now massive, reaching impossibly high into sky.

It was now late afternoon, and the sun was beginning to set. The sunset was casting an eerie red glow on the tower of smoke and ash.

"That's got to be at least 30,000 feet high," said the Pilot.

"We ain't flying over the top of that, we are only at 15,000 feet and already nearly at maximum altitude."

The Pilot let the helicopter hover in place, while the Loadmaster and Gunner joined them to discuss options.

"We have to get the payload to the target," said the Loadmaster, "is there anyway we can fly through the cloud?"

"Negative," said the Pilot.

"That ash will choke out the engines in seconds and we'll drop straight out of the sky."

"Well, that's one way to deliver the package," said the Gunner dryly.

"Does this thing have autopilot?" asked Hardcastle.

"This is one of the newer CH-47's" said the Pilot, "so yeah, I can program in a series of waypoints for it to follow automatically, why?"

"The only way we can deliver the package is to fly directly into that cloud, but that doesn't mean we need to be onboard when it does" said Hardcastle.

The Pilot thought for a moment.

"Screw it, get the device ready. I'll plot a course, get us a little lower, and give us plenty of time to bail out over the lake."

"You ever skydive before?" asked the Loadmaster, pulling out four parachutes.

"A couple times before, yes" said Hardcastle thinking back to the times Honey had talked him into jumping out of perfectly good aircraft.

"Ok, we need to figure out how much time the device needs on the timer" he said.

"I assume this thing is going to drop like a stone when the engines cut out, so maybe we..."

Hardcastle stopped as a screeching sound filled the cabin, like tearing metal.

"What the hell was that?" asked the Loadmaster, standing by the rear loading ramp as he pulled on his parachute.

Over his shoulder, Hardcastle noticed a spot on the closed ramp, it was a dull red colour, distinctly different from the drab olive colour scheme of the rest of the helicopter.

He pondered it a moment, until he noticed it getting brighter, changing from dull red, to bright red, to bright orange, to glowing white.

"LOOK!" was all Hardcastle could say as a flaming paw ripped through the hotspot, into the Loadmaster's back and out through his chest. The intense heat from its claws igniting the man's clothes, as he spat blood across the interior of the helicopter.

The paw retracted through the hole and a gush of freezing cold air rushed in, extinguishing the flaming corpse.

A second later, a massive snout pushed into the hole, plugging the airflow.

The creature began to glow white hot, as it started to push its bulk through the hole.

Not good, Hardcastle's panicked mind raced.

Being stuck in the tight confines of a helicopter at 15,000 feet with one of those things was not going to end well for any of them.

The Grizzly oozed through the hole, the heat from its body and its weight caused the rear ramp to sag. Freezing air rushed into the cabin once more.

Hardcastle noticed the colour of the Grizzly cooling from a bright white to a glowing red, as the cold air rushed in around them.

The Grizzly seemed to be stuck halfway inside, the cold air affecting its ability to transform.

The glowing blob stuck inside the helicopter, contorted and twisted back into the shape of a bear, its massive paws flailing inside the tight confines of the cargo hold.

It growled and roared, showing off gleaming teeth of black obsidian.

Its thrashing was starting to rock the helicopter dangerously.

The Gunner, grabbed the M240 Light Machine Gun from a rack it was stored on, cocked it, then proceeded to fire from the hip directly into the Grizzly's face.

The 7.62mm rounds punched into the creature's rocky head, sending chunks of black rock flying everywhere.

The creature roared and thrashed even harder, as its face disintegrated further and further with each round.

Suddenly, with a mighty tearing noise, the loading ramp broke free completely.

The Grizzly dug its claws into the metal flooring of the helicopter, anchoring itself. The ramp door, still wedged tightly around its body, acted like a parachute, causing a massive amount of drag.

The sudden drag at the back of the helicopter caused the autopilot to over correct. The nose of the helicopter rose sharply, and Hardcastle found himself weightless as the floor dropped from underneath him at a sharp angle.

The Gunner, still holding the bulky weapon, was thrown forwards, down to the back of the helicopter, and towards the Grizzly.

The Grizzly lashed out as the Gunner flew past, raking its claws along the length of his body with such ferocity, it nearly bisected him. His limp corpse plummeting from the Helicopter.

Hardcastle and the Pilot were both thrown forward with equal force.

Hardcastle snagged the netting with one arm, narrowly avoiding falling out the back of the Helicopter, now flying at a 45-degree angle.

The Pilot was launched from the front of the helicopter, and landed in the canoe, now dangling precariously from the winch it was still attached to.

The Pilot was upside down and on his back, his parachute wedged in the front of the boat. He unclipped the straps on his parachute to free himself.

Now free, he righted himself, clinging desperately to the canoe, lest he fall out and into the waiting jaws of death.

The Helicopter continued on its set course towards the volcano. The autopilot trying to correct the wild shifts in weight from the back of the aircraft.

The canoe banged wildly in the turbulence, the Pilot hanging on as if he was riding a bucking bull at a rodeo.

Without warning there was a *TING* sound, as the hook attached to the winch gave way.

Hardcastle watched in horror as the canoe slid down the length of the helicopter, towards the massive drop, towards the Grizzly still trying to drag itself inside.

The Canoe smashed directly into the Grizzly's face. The creature biting down on the boat.

The sudden stop ejected the Pilot, who flew from the boat, rolling over the Grizzly's head, and collided with the ramp still stuck around the creature's midsection.

The impact was enough to dislodge the ramp from the Grizzly, sending both it and the Pilot spiralling into the now blood red evening sky.

With the drag now decreased, the autopilot started to slowly level out the inclined helicopter.

Hardcastle could feel himself getting lightheaded, they were climbing to a higher altitude and the air was getting thinner. Soon he would start becoming hypoxic, losing the mental faculties required to initiate the countdown.

If he didn't do something now, he would either black out and fall to his death, get torn apart by the Grizzly which still struggling with the canoe jammed in its mouth, or if he lasted long enough, he'd fly into a cloud of toxic gas, only to then drop into an erupting volcano.

Pulling himself along the netting on the wall, he dragged himself up the slowly lessening incline, towards the Lodestone device.

The timer still had the previously inputted 2 minutes on the clock. There was no time left and no way to know how far away from the target they were. He had to take a chance they were close enough, so he pushed the initiate button and started the countdown.

The Grizzly still struggling with a face full of canoe, slowly started to drag itself up the metal floor of the helicopter. If it reached the Lodestone, if it damaged it Hardcastle realised, all of this would be for nothing.

Hardcastle's mind flashed to Honey, and to Clayton, and everything they had survived so far, and what was at stake if this plan failed.

He let go.

Sliding along the floor of the helicopter, still flying at an angle, Hardcastle aimed for the canoe.

Striking the back end of the canoe feet first, slamming it further into the jaws of the Grizzly, he felt it give way as the Grizzly, momentarily distracted, lost its grip.

Air rushed past Hardcastle as he flailed through the empty sky.

Reaching and grasping for anything as he tumbled through the air, catching brief glimpses of the helicopter as it rocketed away from him.

Suddenly, his hand touched something, and instinctively closed around it. Pulling himself towards the object in his hand, he realised it was the edge of the canoe, and pulled himself inside.

The rush of air was lessened somewhat, and even in a free fall, he was able to right himself.

He spun around in place, only to find himself staring directly into the raging face of the Grizzly, Canoe wedged firmly in its shattered face.

He was looking right down now and could see the dark waters of Lake Ursa in the fading light of the evening, rapidly rushing up to greet them.

What a way to go, he thought to himself. *At least it should be over quickly.*

Then he saw it.

Wedged at the very end of the canoe, just below where the Grizzly had sunk its teeth in.

Nylon straps flapping in the wind. It was the parachute the Pilot had been wearing, before he was forced to free himself.

Still gripping the edges of the canoe as they plummeted together, Hardcastle inched his way towards the trapped parachute.

Reaching out, he just managed to snag one of the straps, as the Grizzly let out a deep growl that cut through the rushing wind.

The Grizzly started to glow, its face lit up as thousands of tiny cracks turned from red, to orange.

Hardcastle could feel the heat, the air was warming up the further they fell, and the Grizzly was able to shift into a molten state once more.

"Oh no you don't, you're not doing your little jetpack trick," shouted Hardcastle to the creature, "You're going in that lake!"

With a final tug, the parachute flew free, nearly ripping out of Hardcastle's grasp.

Underneath the parachute, something else was wedged at the front of the boat.

Something long and cylindrical.

Thank you, Clayton! thought Hardcastle, as he reached for the nozzle of the liquid nitrogen cannister.

Letting go of the canoe, the parachute in his other hand, he lunged at the release valve on the cannister.

"Hey hothead, you need to chill out!" he shouted into the creature's face, as he cranked open the valve.

The last of the nitrogen sprayed out directly into the Grizzly's mouth. The creature tried to roar, but its rapidly-becoming-molten jaws were now frozen rock solid again, clamped tightly around the front of the canoe.

Hardcastle fell away from the Grizzly and canoe, out into the open sky.

He felt a wave of calm wash over him, as he managed to get the straps of the parachute over his arms, and the clasps snapped shut.

Plummeting towards the lake, he had no idea how close to impact he was. With a deep breath, he grasped around for the ripcord, and pulled.

CHAPTER 15

The parachute snapped open and Hardcastle's rapid descent slowed. He felt like he was flying back up into the sky.

He watched as the thrashing Grizzly sped away from him, towards a watery grave.

Almost as if in slow motion, the beast slammed into the water. A massive splash shot up into the sky, as the canoe splintered apart on impact. The water boiled and hissed as the creature tried in vain to stay afloat, its body rapidly cooling to stone, causing it to sink to the bottom of the lake.

Hardcastle realised how close he had been to hitting the water himself and hoped the parachute had slowed his rate of descent enough for him to survive.

He bent his knees and crossed his arms across his chest, as he braced for impact.

The world became dark and wet once again, as Hardcastle ended up in the lake for the second time. His body was wracked with pain as he hit the water. The air knocked from his lungs, his face stinging like he had just been slapped hard.

He kicked his legs in powerful controlled strokes. They were thankfully not broken like he had anticipated and swept his hands downward as his face pushed towards the surface.

Hardcastle sucked in a lungful of air, as his head broke the surface of the water. He rolled onto his back, kicking with his feet to keep his head afloat, as he struggled with the clasps on the parachute's harness.

He sunk below the water as he wriggled out of the straps. Staring into the inky depths of the lake, he was certain he would see the Grizzly leap out and drag him to his death.

No such thing happened; the creature was now just another rock at the bottom of the lake.

Hardcastle used all his remaining strength to swim to shore. Dragging himself out of the water, he could hear the faint humming of the helicopter off in the distance.

As the sun set, Hardcastle watched as the helicopter reached the massive plume of smoke and ash and disappeared inside. There was a soft bang, and the humming of the engines came to a halt.

Hardcastle stared at the mountain for what felt like an eternity, waiting for some sign that their plan had worked. He looked across the lake towards the town, now lit up as night approached.

The lights across the lake started to dim and flicker.

An orange glow started to illuminate the plume of smoke from below. Rivers of lava ran from the top of the mountain.

A blast of heat erupted from the volcano, dispersing the towering cloud of smoke into a halo around the mountain. Hardcastle could see the air shimmer as a shaft of superheated air vented into the sky.

Lightning bolts snaked through the volcanic clouds, the result of friction from ice particles forming within the cloud, colliding with each other.

The sky was lit up with the discharge of lightning, and the red-hot glow from the mountain.

In an instance, the glow disappeared, and the clouds seemed to fall from the sky. The rivers of lava snaking down the sides of the mountain, quickly lost their colour and solidified into black serpents of glassy obsidian.

The last booms of thunder faded into the night, and then everything was quiet.

Hardcastle saw the headlights of several vehicles speeding towards him.

Colonel Deckard and Honey got out of the lead vehicle and made their way towards him.

"You made it!" shouted Honey as she threw her arms around him.

Her warmth made Hardcastle realise how cold he was.

It felt like a there was a distinct chill in the air, but it could just be the adrenalin wearing off.

"You sure put on one hell of a fireworks display" said the Colonel, clapping a hand on Hardcastle's shoulder, "just in time for the 4th of July."

"Colonel Deckard" said Hardcastle, "I'm sorry, your men didn't make it."

The smile dropped from his face as the Colonel looked at Hardcastle sternly and nodded his head.

"We'll make sure everyone knows of their sacrifice."

"Thank you, Professor," he said extending his hand.

"Did it work?" asked Hardcastle as he shook his hand.

"Satellites measured a massive spike in temperature, before it dropped significantly," said Honey.

"The temperature inside the volcano got as low as -450 degrees. All the lava has turned into obsidian, resolidifying and reinforcing the plug."

"And what of the creature?" said the Colonel, "we lost track of it once you both fell from the helicopter."

"It met a *grizzly end...*" said Hardcastle with a smirk as he looked out across the lake.

A few more army jeeps started to arrive on the scene. Soldiers started to secure the area.

"What were you going to tell me earlier?" Hardcastle said, looking into Honey's eyes.

"Honey!!" shouted a voice, as a man ran from one of the newly arrived jeeps, swept her up in his arms, and as he placed his hands on her face, kissed her.

"Tom!" Honey shouted in surprise; a mixture of emotions flashed across her face.

"I thought you were still on deployment for another 6 months?" she said.

"I know, I know," said the man, "but I was in an accident... my helo went down while I was on a mission, I'm okay though, just a few minor injuries, a few fractures, *burns...*"

The Colonel clapped the man on the shoulder, "They sure make 'em tough, don't they?" he said.

"I'm sorry Captain, that I wasn't able to inform you of the Major's return sooner, but we agreed it was vital for you to stay on task."

Hardcastle stood there wearing a look of shock.

Honey turned to him and slowly said "Radford, this is Tom... my husband."

"Ah, the famous professor I've heard so much about," said the man, extending his hand warmly.

"It's a pleasure to finally meet you Radford."

"I'm Tom...Tom Svenning."

Hardcastle said a hasty farewell to Honey and painfully made his way over to a waiting ambulance.

As the medics checked him over and assessed his injuries, he thought about the future. He no doubt would be busy for the foreseeable future, now he had been given full access to study the mountain.

"Is it me or is it suddenly cold?" said one of the medics, her breath visible in the night air.

Hardcastle stared at the now dormant volcano and pondered the ramifications of their actions stopping the eruption.

He started to shiver, as a cold wind blew from across the lake, and it gently started to snow.